AVERY COLT
IS A SNAKE, A THIEF, A LIAR

RON A. AUSTIN

AVERY COLT
IS A SNAKE, A THIEF, A LIAR

RON A. AUSTIN

SOUTHEAST MISSOURI STATE UNIVERSITY PRESS | 2019

AVERY COLT IS A SNAKE, A THIEF, A LIAR BY RON A. AUSTIN

COPYRIGHT 2019: RON A. AUSTIN
SOFTCOVER: $18.00

FIRST PUBLISHED IN 2019 BY
SOUTHEAST MISSOURI STATE UNIVERSITY PRESS
ONE UNIVERSITY PLAZA, MS 2650
CAPE GIRARDEAU, MO 63701
WWW.SEMOPRESS.COM

COVER DESIGN: IAN O'NEILL

LIBRARY OF CONGRESS

NAMES: AUSTIN, RON A., AUTHOR.
TITLE: AVERY COLT IS A SNAKE, A THIEF, A LIAR / RON AUSTIN.
DESCRIPTION: CAPE GIRARDEAU, MO : SOUTHEAST MISSOURI STATE UNIVERSITY PRESS,
    2019.
IDENTIFIERS: LCCN 2018045709 | ISBN 9781732039919
CLASSIFICATION: LCC PS3601.U86354 A6 2019 | DDC 813/.6--DC23

LC RECORD AVAILABLE AT HTTPS://LCCN.LOC.GOV/2018045709

Store Owner Wounds Two Of Gang Of Armed Robbers

By Margaret Gillerman
Of the Post-Dispatch Staff

The owner of a small store in north St. Louis shot two of 12 armed youths who were attempting to rob him over the weekend, police said.

One 17-year-old was critically wounded when Frank Laskley, the owner of the Three L Food Shop at 3101 Cass Avenue, opened fire on the gang. The youth was shot several times in the right arm, abdo men and back.

Police had not located the other wounded youth, but found blood outside the shop, according to Officer Jeffrey Souders, who handled the case.

The incident began when the gang entered the small confectionery and barbecue shop at 11:30 p.m. Saturday. Laskley, 59, told police the youths, ages 16 to 20, were carrying knives and one appeared to be carrying a gun.

Laskley told police that the youth he shot had jumped over the counter and knocked Laskley's wife, Flora, 51, to the floor. The youth then opened the cash register and took $11.

Souders said that six or eight of the youths, flourishing knives, then had jumped Laskley. "Laskley pushed them back, grabbed his .38 revolver and opened fire," Souders said.

Laskley shot the one youth at least five times and the other youth was shot once.

Souders said Laskley reopened the shop immediately after the incident. Laskley, who lives in the 3200 block of University Street, usually barbecues all night on weekends, Souders said.

Earlier Saturday night before the incident, the youths had thrown bricks at a bus at North Grand Boulevard and Bell Avenue, breaking a window, Souders said.

The youths also had assaulted an older man at Grand and Dr. Martin Luther King Drive, witnesses said. The man refused to speak with police, Souders said.

Antonio Johnson of the 4700 block of Aldine Place, was in serious condition today in the intensive care unit at St. Louis University Hospitals.

The youth was admitted to the hospital in critical condition.

The Laskleys also operate a self-service laundry next door to the food shop.

Mrs. Laskley said today that they have been robbed several times and this time she knew most of the youths as being from the neighborhood.

"The police aren't doing anything to round them up," she said. "If that's the way police handle this, how are we ever going to make it stop?"

For Frank, Flora, and the Three L Food Shop

"It's like they all forgot, man. Nobody care about us.
That why we always end up in prison instead of college,
Living in the system working kitchen for chump change,
Lost in the streets, niggas playing that gun game,
Where nobody wins—just a bunch of mamas losing.
Dead body in the field, nobody heard the shooting.
We living in the streets where the options is limited,
'Cause its burnt buildings instead of jobs and businesses."

"Fields." Danny Brown.

"Am I worth it? Did I put enough work in?"
"Sing About Me." Kendrick Lamar.

"OUR GENERATION POSSESSES ONLY A CURSORY SENSE OF THE WORLD OUR ANCESTORS BRAVED THOUGH THE BURDENS OF HISTORY BEAR UNMOVABLY UPON US."

ANNOTATIONS, JOHN KEENE.

CONTENTS

ACKNOWLEDGEMENTS

Selected stories in this work were previously published in the following: "Do It Yourself" in *Black Warrior Review* 39.1 (2012); "The Gatecrasher of Hyboria" in *Natural Bridge* 30 (2013); "Snakes, Thieves, Liars" in *Draft Horse Summer* (2013); "The Garden of Fire and Blood" in *Gulf Stream Literary Magazine* #10 (2013); "Shine" in *The Masters Review New Voices* (2015); "Neck Bones" in *Ninth Letter* 12.1 (2015); "Cut Open the Vein and All You'll Find Is Rust" in *Cog* 1 (2015); "Most Valuable Player" in *Tahoma Literary Review* 7 (2016); "Cauldron" in *Story Quarterly* 49 (2017); "Nobody Promised Milk and Honey" in *Big Muddy* 18.2 (2018); and "Teeth's Story" in *Juked Magazine* (2018).

PART I

DO IT YOURSELF

BABY POSSUMS SQUIRMED and squealed in a nest of splinters and pulp. They curled into big Cs like overcooked prawns. Wispy fur covered pink bodies. Solid black eyes slit open. Teeth and claws had just begun to point, curve. I reached to pick one up, but Mama Possum punched dingy paws into hardwood floor, bristled fur into rows of white needles, and bared tiny, arrowhead teeth—this possum wasn't playing possum at all.

I stomped, swatted a broom at her, told her to get the hell out, but she didn't startle, she didn't jump. She just wasn't going to be intimidated by a stumpy, nine-year-old kid who couldn't fall asleep without the television's cold, blue glow.

Gremlins thrive in darkness. One light bulb blinks out and then—SCRUNCH! A scaly hand is squeezing your throat, and all you can do is gurgle help—at least that's what my older sister Danielle had told me. We called her Yell for short, cuz that's all she ever did.

Mama Possum strutted around the attic, like she owned it, only leased it for the winter months, her fat tail swishing behind her like a length of coil. I ran to tell Mom about the possum and found her in the kitchen stroking a hot comb through Yell's hair. Mom yanked it from nappy and matted to straight and silken. Smoke rolled off Yell's scalp. This heavy, funky smell underscored the death of something delicate. I heard brambly snags ripping from all the way across the room. But Yell didn't fuss or fidget. She just worked a red crayon in a tattered old Care Bear coloring book, her face smooth as creamy peanut butter.

"Hey y'all, there's a big, fat, ugly possum up in the attic," I announced. "We gonna call an exterminator to poison that thing?"

"Nuh-unh. Those folks are crooks," Mom said. "I called Animal Control last time a stray cat got in the basement." The hot comb got caught in a stubborn patch of Yell's hair. Mom yanked hard. Yell's eyes glassed over. "The man came and parked right out front with one of those tacky vans—you know the ones with the bars over the windows—and he went down there with his snare and strangled that cat, strung her right up. That thing was possessed, snarling and hissing and spitting. You know what that man told me?"

I shook my head no. Yell stabbed her crayon into her coloring book. Mom pointed the hot comb at me.

"That man told me I could take him out through the front if you don't mind the neighbors seeing, or I could take him through the back, if you might help me out with a little tip." Mom pressed her lips into a scar and attacked Yell's hair. "Twenty dollars? Twenty dollars! Does that sound like a little tip to you?"

I didn't know what to say, so I shrugged. Mom calmed down a bit, finished hot-combing a few snags, and handed Yell a silver vanity mirror.

Yell smiled at herself and then frowned just as quick. "Mama, you gotta get closer to the scalp or there'll be all this frizz. I don't want a lick of frizz."

Mom sighed and went back to work. "But Avery, you could probably lure that possum out with one of those rotten bananas you like to keep in the back of the fridge. Bang a pot real loud and run her out. I don't know. Do something."

"Yeah, Avery, do something," Yell echoed Mom.

I was about to ask why me, but then I thought about how Mom's designer belt would whip and emblazon my thighs with welts in stylish patterns, cheetah print for back talking, snakeskin for contemptuous eye rolls and haughty body language. Besides, killing rodents was clearly catalogued as man's work in the family bible of household duties.

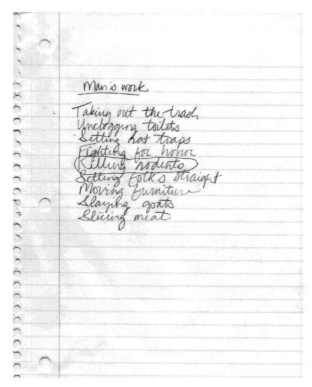

Man's work

Taking out the trash
Unclogging toilets
Setting rat traps
Fighting for honor
Killing rodents
Setting folk's straight
Moving furniture
Slaying goats
Slicing meat

So I took a pot and a ladle and a brown banana too. I got to the foot of the steps before images of Mama Possum's yellow teeth flashed in my head. I saw her teeth sinking through my pump-up sneakers; her teeth tearing tendons, rending fat; her teeth pink with blood, my toes ground to hamburger.

I fought the sudden urge to pee and retreated down the steps. By the time I got back to the kitchen, Mom had called Grandma and Granddad at the corner store. Mom folded her arms and grunted, "Mama, what do you want me to do?"

Granddad and Grandma had bought the family home by sweltering over pans of hot grease and feeding folks they didn't always like. Me, Mom, Dad, and Yell lived on the second floor. Granddad and Grandma lived on the first, though some nights they preferred sleeping on cots in the back of the corner store, fearful that neighborhood thieves would break in at night and steal a fortune of lamb shanks, hot pickles, and industrial kitchen equipment. They were too broke for an alarm system and didn't trust cops to protect what they owned.

Now if the basement flooded, or the floorboards rotted, or roaches invaded walls and crawl spaces, Grandma raged and blamed it on us for being trifling. Mom never liked having to call Grandma at work to break bad news.

Mom always squeezed the receiver tight and chewed her lip raw. This time she said, "Mama. Mama—you're not listening. I said I told that boy to do it, but you know how he is. You can't tell him nothing. Unh-hunh. Mmm-hmm. Toughen up? What you think I've been doing? He's soft as pudding and I-don't-know-what-else. Well, you're welcome to give it a try. And—say what? No, Mama, the man of the house is not here. And you know that. I had to put his ass out yet again.

"I don't care if he is my husband—who needs a gambling mooch? Say what you want, but I don't need him. Come again? Oh, hush up. The kids will learn, now could you please put Daddy on the phone? Thank you.

"Daddy, yes—yes, but could you come get this possum? Okay, I told him to, but do y'all listen? Just c'mon on and get it done. Mm-hmm. What you mean I won't like the way you do it? It doesn't matter—long as you do it." Mom looked down and saw me standing there. She turned away from me and whispered something into the receiver. "Uh-huh, alright, I know. Thank you."

"MAMA SAY YOU as yellow as that banana used to be!" Yell shouted. She was sitting on my bed and scribbling in her coloring book with a blue crayon, her shiny new hair up in a neat ponytail. I was eating the supposed-to-be-bait banana. That banana turned to mealworm mush when Yell said YELLOW. "She say you yellow as mustard. Yellow as a little fluffy, baby chick. Yellow as—"

"Shut up already!"

"Oh, baby boy, did I hurt hims feelings?"

Yell never had to do anything hard. Not for real. She played piano, danced ballet, pranced in leotards, whirled satin streamers through air, and I was damn jealous. So I snatched her legs, whipped her off my bed. Her butt hit the floor with a satisfying thud.

"Ow, that hurt!" She growled and raked my shins with her knuckles.

"Ow, that hurt!" I growled and yanked her up into a half nelson (I mean, almost a half nelson—she had three years and a freakish six inches on me).

I wrestled her through the door, out into the hall. She turned, faced me, and kept right on talking with her fists on hips she didn't have. "You yellow as a egg yolk! You yellow as baby shit!" I slammed the door in her face, but I could still hear her taunting YELL-LOW! YELL-LOW! YELL-LOW!

I opened her coloring book, wanting to scrawl a monstrous dick over Funshine bear's belly badge. But I paused and considered the slashes of red crayon jagging across each page. That hot-combing must've hurt so bad she couldn't even color between the lines. She took the pain and tranced out, kind of like those tribal dudes who can take a steel spike through both cheeks and smile. I hated to admit it, but in a lot of ways my big sister was tough, much tougher than my yellow ass.

Toughness was an heirloom passed down by Granddad. Diabetes made his eyes milky and his muscles slack, but sick or not, he could still make screws tight with one twist of his wrist. He could still work twelve hours at the family corner store, slaughter a hog, blow flames out of hot coals—if he didn't, who would? Necessity destroyed the most vulnerable parts of him and gave him iron strength in return.

Granddad was old school and believed in extreme self-reliance. He had no problem getting a goddamn possum out of the attic, even if that meant shooting it dead with his World War II service revolver. He sat in the kitchen loading his revolver while Mom tried to convince him death by one-man firing squad wasn't a real form of pest control.

"Daddy, that is animal cruelty. You cannot." She told him as she hunched over the Yellow Pages, pretending to look for a legitimate exterminator.

"Can't do what?" Granddad took a bullet out of a mason jar and slid it into the chamber. "Kill a big goddamn rat?" Two, three, four more bullets slid in the chamber, Granddad's arthritic hands surprisingly lithe. "You know possums used to eat babies—one nearly ate you, Cheryl." He spun the cylinder. It clicked like a card in bicycle spokes: *TAT-TAT-TAT*. "Now what you call that? People cruelty?"

"No, but I call what you're doing country as all-get-out."

"I'd chase the damn thing with a brick if my knees weren't gone." Granddad slapped the revolver's cylinder shut and winked at me. Yell stood next to me, her body tight with the same kind of excitement she got from watching neighborhood boys slap box over scuffed sneakers.

Mom didn't want me and Yell seeing all that violence, but we crouched by the landing and heard it. Granddad walked up to the attic. The steps groaned the same way old women do on hot days. His breaths were heavy and blunt as wind beating against a window. A few more footsteps, a long pause, and then scuffling, claws scraping hardwood. There was hissing, papers flapping, cursing, clattering, banging, and then there was a *POP! POP!* like Fourth of July fireworks, but it was early June, and the sky didn't light up. Dogs moaned and barked, but no one screamed. Gunshots on a summer night in our neighborhood were natural and mundane as R&B on Saturday mornings, cicadas screeching at dusk.

Granddad came back down those steps with a black trash bag held high in his hand. He was sweating and smiling, triumphant like he had just bagged a prize boar. Mama Possum's face poked through a hole in the trash bag, her eyes crossed into cartoon Xs. Blood frosted the white hair around her snout. Her earthworm tongue lolled out like *so fucking what.*

I looked up at Granddad and saw how old age fit him like a dowdy, two-piece tuxedo: short in the sleeves, tight in the gut, unflattering in the butt. Mom cradled Yell's head and performed her most earnest stage shriek. "Daddy! Get that damn thing out of here! I mean it—I'll be sick. You don't want that mess on your shoes."

But the job wasn't done. After Granddad chucked Mama Possum in the dumpster, he put all three baby possums in an old shoebox, grabbed a wire hanger, and beckoned me into the bathroom. He told me, "C'mon, boy, give me a hand."

Afraid of his plans for those possums, that hanger, and me, I smarted off and asked, "You don't need help peeing, do you?"

"Boy, I swear I'd beat the brakes off you if I thought it'd help any."

Yell skipped down the hallway and whipped a baton threaded with satin streamers. The fabric flew behind her in red and blue whorls. I tried to snatch her hand but couldn't catch her. I would've let Mom take that hot comb and burn my earlobes crispy as pork rinds rather than hurt anybody, anything.

MOM HAD JUST cleaned the bathroom. The wall and floor tiles were scrubbed creamy white. The toilet bowl water rippled in waves of unsettling blue. Decorative soaps lined the windowsill like stones. Everything smelled artificial green. Granddad sat on the edge of the tub and bent that hanger. The box of baby possums jittered between his boots. "We'll drown these suckers before we lay them with they mammy."

I was dumb enough to ask him, "Why?"

"Suppose these suckers get to chirping and squeaking and another possum—uglier and meaner then that one I put a bullet in—comes into the house looking for a fight?" Granddad shaped the frame of the hanger into handles. "Possums got no manners, you have to understand that." Granddad set the hanger by his side and let his fingers rest for a moment. He looked down at me, his eyes hard but not unkind. "You can beat a man and teach him some respect." Granddad looked away and twisted the hook of the hanger into a tiny noose. "But a beast? He won't learn nothing, not rodents anyway—damn sure not a possum." Granddad pinched the first possum by his shoestring tail. "Now watch."

The possum screeched and wriggled but couldn't keep that wire noose off his neck. Granddad twisted the wire tighter and dunked the possum in. The possum struggled, scrambled up the slick interior of the toilet bowl only to slide back into that cold water. Unsettling blue soaked his fur, dripped down his snout. Granddad pressed him to the bottom and flushed. I closed my eyes and counted. *ONE MISSISSIPPI. TWO MISSISSIPPI. THREE MISSISSIPPI. FOUR MISSISSIPPI. FIVE MISSISSIPPI. SIX MISSISSIPPI.*

I opened my eyes, and that possum was gray, floating snout up. "Go on," Granddad said and handed me the hanger. My nerves splintered. Sweat crawled along my hairline. The hanger vibrated in my hand. I pinched a possum by his slick, muscular tail. As I tried to work the noose around his neck, the possum snapped his head up and bit me in my thumb. His teeth were no bigger than the points of thumb tacks, but they hurt like full-grown fangs. I chomped my tongue not to scream.

I dropped the possum, and he hit the tile with a wet *THWAK*. He tried to crawl away, but Granddad blocked him with a boot. My blood stained those creamy white tiles. Granddad groaned and said, "Awww hell."

"HOLD STILL," MOM told me as she dabbed my thumb with alcohol. "Look at you, you're gonna get thirty-something shots in the stomach for acting a fool."

Pain from the possum bite drained and was replaced by fear that I'd turn into a strange beast. I looked out the kitchen window and saw myself running through the alley on all fours, red foam bubbling from my mouth, coarse fur sprouting from my back and shoulders, my pupils narrowed to feral slits.

"That possum wasn't but five minutes from between his mammy's legs. Ain't no way he had a touch of rabies," Granddad said.

"You don't know that." She shook her head and rifled through a few cabinets and then shouted, "Where are the Band-Aids?" She stomped off into the hall. "Danielle! What did you do with the damn Band-Aids?"

With Mom gone, Granddad pulled a pint of whiskey out of his back pocket. He poured it into a tablespoon, pushed it to my lips, told me, "Medicine."

I held my nose and gulped it down. This bitter metallic taste surged over my tongue and tonsils. That liquor scorched my throat and the lining of my stomach like turpentine, then settled into an uncomfortable pocket of heat.

Mom came back flapping a few Teenage Mutant Ninja Turtle Band-Aids in her hand. She stopped dead at the doorway and told me, "Avery, you better not." My stomach grunted. Her eyes flared. She looked to Granddad. "Daddy, tell him."

"Boy, don't—" But I did. I puked all over Granddad, all over his khakis and soot stained button up. Granddad slapped a chunk of undigested banana off his chest and said, "Can't even hold a swallow of whiskey...."

"A swallow of what, Daddy?" Mom said. "A swallow of what?"

FALLING ASLEEP THAT night I sketched the scene of Granddad killing Mama Possum on soft spots in my mind. I couldn't articulate it back then, but I was beginning to learn how anxiety could hijack the circuitry in my brain and redraw the world in wobbling, surreal lines. The possum was a giant clump of dust. Her pink claws curled under her body like the clawed feet under our porcelain bathtub. Granddad's head was a stone stacked on top of a totem, toggling as he boxed the possum in a corner. He cocked the gun's hammer, fingered the trigger, aimed, shot. Fire flashed from the muzzle, smoke zigged out in blue streamers. The bullet flew, a fat, black beetle. It hit Mama Possum. She burst into inconsequential tufts of doll hair. No bone, no blood. Those baby possums swirled in a silver bowl and dissolved into color like dye pellets do on Easter.

GRANDDAD HADN'T COMPLETELY forgiven me for wussing out on the possum executions and barfing up his good whiskey. It wasn't apology enough to have scrubbed his clothes with an old washing board until my hands shriveled like a mummy's, but I had to do chores at the dumb-ass corner store too. Before the business soured, neighborhood folks had lunch at the corner store daily. You could tell where they were from by what they ordered. Oldheads and respectable elders who lived near the water tower survived on cheap cuts of soul food nobody else wanted: braised neck bones, tripe, snoot sandwiches. Truckers and construction workers coming from the industrial district on North Broadway wanted cold sandwiches stacked with roast beef, salami, and cheese. Grown folks from the lounges on Grand needed grease on their stomachs to soak up liquor and beer. They ordered anything fried: fish, chicken, okra. Grandma always growled *Batter a boot and them drunk bastards will eat it, sho'll will.* Kids from around the block just wanted freeze pops and candy bars, anything that'd make their teeth ache.

Folks loved the corner store. But I used to hate it so bad. Granddad and Grandma always put me to work sweeping ashes out of the smoker, washing grit out of collard greens, sponging pig's blood off the butcher's table. I didn't understand that years later, after the corner store was nothing but weeds and rubble, I'd still smell ancient charcoal smoke on my skin, feel grit under my fingernails, see my palms stained with blood, and succumb to a crippling grief, the kind that closes over you like wings, eclipses the best days.

GRANDDAD HAD ME collect apple wood for the smoker as part of my punishment. I didn't mind because it gave me an excuse to climb trees and spy on the neighborhood. The heat outside was set on broil. Sunlight dribbled thick enough to rub between two fingers. I scrambled up a tall, stout apple tree and perched deep in the boughs, back where the bark was scaly. Fifteen feet above ground, I twisted my hands into a pirate's telescope, squinted, and surveyed North St. Louis.

Abandoned buildings crumbled on the horizon, brawny frames and bricks disintegrating into pulp and red dust. At the corner of Cass and Bacon, Miss Annette manned her snack cart: dipped green apples in sugary sludge, popped popcorn, spun cotton candy. Shirtless and wiry, Iron Joe pushed his shopping cart through an alleyway. Scraps of metal and shoes tumbled out of the cart onto the cobblestone. His obsidian skin sopped up that rich sunlight. I swear I could hear the rusty wheels on his cart squalling *SQUEE-EAK. SQUEE-EAK. SQUEE-EAK.*

Two badass kids, Russell and Cameron, swaggered down the street toward my perch. Russell snapped a bandana at stray cats. Cameron slugged imaginary enemies with a solid wood baseball bat. Mom had warned me to stay far away from older boys like them, as if I'd catch clusters of oozing sores. As if they could touch my skin and turn me to a gremlin.

One time I overheard her talking bad about them to a mean, goat-bearded old gossip. The goat-bearded woman said *Cameron and his little cousin, you know they ain't no good. They'd spit on you soon as setting eyes on you. Mm-hmm. I heard they stomped on Frank's nephew over two dollars and a pack of cigarettes—I ain't lying. Goddamn petty. And you know both they mamas got hooked on that stuff. It's a damn shame how folks let they whole house go up in smoke.*

I recalibrated my pirate's telescope and turned my attention to a lot where a crew of day laborers shone bright with sweat. They thrust rusted shovels into dark dirt and hacked down browned evergreen shrubs with machetes. They must have been drunk or high because they were clowning on each other in between machete whacks. Their insults boomed.

WHAM! You non-bathing-ass-dirty-drawers-wearin muthafucka. WHAM! Fuck that with your old stanky-breath-raw-chitlin-eating-ass. WHAM! Oh you a old-lumpy-sweet-potato-dick havin' nigga!

Laughing with machetes at their sides, the day laborers were something like the Masai warriors I read about in National Geographic, but without the red robes, the bead necklaces, the aura of honor. *WHAM!* A gardener missed the shrub he was aiming for and hit a juneberry tree. Black fruit rained from the branches, splashed his shoulders.

Granddad never picked juneberries from trees around the neighborhood. He claimed you could taste exhaust, choke on gravel in the seed. Me and him used to pick them from a clearing in East St. Louis, near Eads Bridge where small islands of land were never molested by industry—at least that's what we did when he wasn't disappointed in me for being yellow.

"You bitch-ass-pork-butt-lickin'-ass-dude," I said as I karate chopped a dry branch off the apple tree. "You stupid-scabies-munchin'-ass-dude." The strike hurt me worse than it did the tree. My hands were too soft, fresh and pruny as the rump of a newborn rodent. I chopped off another branch. A painful, watery blister swelled on the side of my palm. I wanted it to pop and harden into a callus like the ones on Granddad's hands. I hit harder.

I started working on another branch, but it was knobby, thick as a club, and wouldn't fall easily. I closed a fist and hammered it, yelling, "You yellow-pussy-ass-smurf-kissing-ass—" *CRIIICK!* The knobby branch snapped and crashed onto the sidewalk below, right at Cameron's feet.

"Hey!" he shouted. "That's some punk shit!"

I withdrew into the tree limbs, concealed myself in the bark and bloom. Cameron threw rocks but couldn't reach me. Russell tugged his sleeve and said, "C'mon, cuz, quit playing."

Cameron swatted a dismissive hand at me, slung that bat over his shoulder, and turned away. Russell asked Cameron, "Bruh, you hungry?"

"N'all, I ain't hungry."

"You trippin'—I'm hungry den a mug."

"You better drink some water and tighten up."

"I ain't no bum, nigga."

"I never said you was, nigga."

"You trippin'. Let's go."

THE BELL ABOVE the corner store door rang as I elbowed my way into the lobby. Grandma was in the kitchen stirring something in a large pot, maybe cabbage by the faintly sour smell. Steam formed a halo around her head. Her hair was silver, black, and knotted like well-used steel wool. Granddad was taking a stab at a Sunday crossword puzzle, a pair of tarnished, gold-framed glasses he saved from the trash low on his nose.

"Firewood's here!" I boomed. A strange sense of pride exploded in my chest. I had done something right. No one could deny me that. I felt strong. Those branches were light in my arms.

Granddad took the glasses off his nose and told me, "Fire's dead. Fire's been dead. Can't burn no fire if you ain't got no wood." Granddad flapped the paper at me. "Don't you know that, Avery? Don't you know nothing?"

I could've jabbed a twig through his eye and out the back of his dumb, craggy skull. I dropped the wood and walked away, picking at the tender blisters on my hand.

"Boy, you need to come back here and pick up these damn sticks! Avery!" Last time Granddad had to raise his voice with me, I was saddled up on a Daffy Duck inflatable for two days. I kept walking, aching to karate chop a full-grown tree until every bone in my hand broke.

The bell above the door rang again. Cameron and Russell hustled through the door. Close up, those kids looked almost tough. Blurry tattoos of names and numbers marked their chests and necks. Skull-shaped buckles bucked off their belts. They mean-mugged as if the muscles responsible for half-smiles had been severed. But they were still kids, smooth-faced and smooth-muscled, even the dark bags under their eyes looked like stage makeup.

Russell attacked the snack rack. He pocketed Skor candy bars and Mallomars, tore into bags of barbecue chips. Cameron paced the store and tapped his bat on the twenty-five-cent toy machine, on the comic book rack, on me.

Grandma barely looked up from her cutting board. She beheaded a fish with a dead *THUNK!* Granddad folded his paper and placed his glasses in his breast pocket before asking the kids, "Need something?"

Russell didn't say a word. He sucked flavoring off his fingers and smacked his lips. Cameron slung that bat over his shoulder, posed like an action movie badass, and said, "N'all. We good."

Granddad didn't trip. He just squinted at Cameron and said, "I didn't ask you how you was. I don't care if you good. I asked if you needed something."

Russell got in Granddad's face and yelled, "You better sit your old ass down somewhere before you get fucked up!" Russell would've been intimidating if his voice hadn't cracked. Cameron flanked Granddad and raised his bat high.

Granddad shot his arm up at an angle and deflected the bat, a technique I figured he must've learned from a stony karate master in Okinawa. There was this dense *THUNK.* An oil-black bruise instantly slicked across Granddad's forearm. But he didn't look hurt or even mad. His face was perfectly empty when he wrenched the bat out of Cameron's hand and headbutted him in the nose. Cameron staggered back and sputtered *FUCK! FUCK! FUCK!* Every drop of boldness he had leaked out of him, darkening lines in the linoleum. I couldn't believe so much blood could gush out of a human nose.

Russell feigned a few jabs, too timid to commit. He took a bat swing to the chest and a bat swing to the groin for his trouble, then crumpled on the floor like a dead roach. Granddad's movements were stiff but economical, governed by inertia and the knowledge of how spirits will break under enough force.

Cameron's eyes widened big and glossy, full of innocent shock. He couldn't have expected such stubborn wrath from a mean, old goat. Granddad slammed the bat into Cameron's knee and there was a dry, hollow *CRICK*! Cameron cried out. Granddad dropped the bat, put a hand over his mouth, and laid him gently on the floor with the same motions a country preacher might use to dunk a sinner in a river.

Granddad leaned a hand on the wall and steadily kicked those kids in the ribs and chest. They whimpered. Granddad wheezed, but he kept kicking with an intensely bored sag in his face, like he was only scrubbing floorboards, caulking grout. He'd looked more thrilled when he had killed that possum the other day.

An angry sizzle popped in the kitchen. Unfazed, Grandma continued to fry fish for the dinner rush she hoped would come later.

A couple of kicks to the head, and those kids were out. Either that or pretending, silently praying he'd stop. Granddad nudged them both with his toe. Neither one fluttered an eyelid. Satisfied, he took a cigarette out of his breast pocket and lit it with shaking hands. He took a long drag, burnt half the cigarette to ashes. He coughed wet, wrenching coughs, the kind of coughs that make your throat sore just by listening. I heard rusty nails and bolts rattling in his lungs. Once his hacking fit was over, he looked at me and said, "Well, damn. Boy, you gonna get a mop or just sit there gawking?"

I mopped where Cameron bled everywhere, the smell of iron powerful in my nose. By the time I finished, those kids had sat up and huddled together, dazzled with pain. They ran cautious hands over newly tender spots and winced. With their faces swollen and clothes soiled, those kids looked realer somehow, more genuine, like Granddad had beaten them into being. He wasn't done. *TAT-TAT-TAT*—the revolver cylinder spun behind me.

Granddad plopped down in front of Russell and Cameron and placed the gun in his lap. He stared them down for so long I thought they might turn to salt. Finally, Granddad lifted the gun, tapped the muzzle on Cameron's forehead, and shouted *BLAOW!* Granddad shouted again as he gave Russell the same. *BLAOW!* Crazier than anything else, those kids didn't dare jump or holler. They just accepted the gun in their faces, like it was a benediction.

"Try me again—" Granddad stopped to hack some more, this time spitting reddish-yellow phlegm into a napkin. "Try me again, and bet I don't put a hole in your face." The kids nodded. There wasn't anything else to do.

Having said his peace, Granddad pushed himself off the floor, grimacing with trouble from his hips. The kids looked at each other and then rose warily, ready to duck a hook, a haymaker.

Granddad asked them, "Can you talk?"

The kids nodded their heads yes.

"Can you walk?"

Russell ventured a stuttering, "Yes."

"Good. Now walk your sorry asses outta here."

GRANDDAD TOOK ME to pick juneberries later that day. Ornery snapping turtles protected the clearing and attacked our shoes, their heads flying off spring-loaded necks, their beaks sharp as wire cutters. We fed those turtles wilted lettuce and soggy tomato slices, humble offerings. They sank back into the scummy pond, nothing but strange, ornate stones stirred from the silt.

In time, I'd learn that Granddad wasn't famous for his work ethic, or his command over coals, or his covenant with machinery—n'all. He was known for handing out good, country ass-whoopings. I had heard about it, but I hadn't seen it before that day. I had just the right balance of curiosity and dread to ask, "Granddad, would you shoot them kids, for real?"

Granddad didn't answer right away. He sucked in his cheeks and thought. I wanted him to say *n'all I sho'll wouldn't—they just needed a good scare.* But he told me, "I sho'll would."

Granddad said that, and I closed my eyes. I saw bullets shredding the flesh under Mama Possum's fur. I saw the lungs inside those baby possums bursting with blue water. I saw Granddad tapping that gun on foreheads, faces cracking like eggshells. I saw Granddad coughing up nails and corroded razor blades. All the rust in his lungs.

He told me, "One day you're walking, talking, eating, shitting, and then you stop. Lay down dead like this stump." He picked up a log filled with white, writhing termites. "Get filled with bugs the same way too. If some want that sooner than others, I don't mind helping. It's the polite thing to do." He hurled the log far over the treetops.

Traitorous tears slipped from my eyes. I couldn't sleeve them away quick enough. "Awwww, boy, you asked me a question, and I gave you an answer." Granddad said. He slapped a rough, warm hand on the back of my neck. "Now would you please shut the hell up before I give you something to howl about."

I knew better than to keep on. I looked up at those juneberry branches stretching long against a red, dusk sky. They made the kind of switches that cut deep and keep you quiet.

THE GATECRASHER OF HYBORIA

MR. DUNN ONLY threatened to flunk me out of fourth grade because he didn't like the way I talked—at least that was what I was going to tell my parents. I didn't have a lisp or a cleft palate or a stutter—and I wasn't slow either—but I said *Y'ALL* and *N'ALL* and *SHO'LL IS* and *SHO'LL AIN'T*.

The dialect I spoke at ten years old was three licks neighborhood slang, two licks swear words Mom and Dad used when no one important was listening, and one lick southern drawl I gleaned from neighborhood elders gossiping on brick porches. That chop-shop dialect coated my throat like mucous, muffled my vowel sounds, made all my consonants roll lazily off my tongue. I loved that Midwest slang. But Mr. Dunn sho'll didn't.

As a teacher at Holy Cross Lutheran—a southside St. Louis private school for those who were plenty God fearing and pious but too poor to afford Catholic school—Mr. Dunn believed it was his duty to carve fatty hunks of hardened lower classness out of gelatinous, juvenile minds.

He told pink-eared white boys to stop saying *I seen him* instead of *I saw him* and lumping Big League Chew in their bottom lips like it was tobacco dip. He kept cords of bungee rope to cinch the sagging pants of burgeoning gang bangers. He begged Vietnamese kids to quit yowling like cats caught in a garbage disposal. He suggested Charu Fatima Bhatnagar adopt a sensible nickname like Nicole or Sarah for future job applications and resumes.

Mr. Dunn was a righteous crusader who crushed different cultures into a bland, monotone paste. In his gospel, assimilation was salvation. Even though I had mastered every Hooked On Phonics module and could speak Standard American English when I wanted, I chose to be an unclean heretic. Years later I'd be punished for my hubris by the fickle Gods of Language who jammed my code-switching-switch on "white-boy," so sometimes black folks looked at me like a stranger or worse, an enemy spy, when I wheedled *what's up* in thin, sanitized tones.

Language Arts became a daily inquisition. I knew Mr. Dunn wanted to hang me from a ceiling fan, strap leather-bound dictionaries and thesauruses to my ankles, let me swing until either I enunciated vowels clearly or my kneecaps popped. But I refused to be censored. I refused to enunciate every vowel when it was my turn to read out loud, just so I could see the scraggly, night crawler veins plump in his forehead.

One time I read, "Ben bit into the GREE-SEE hamburger."

"Avery, it's not GREE-SEE, but GR-EASY. GRRR-EASY," Mr. Dunn coached me, pulling his lips away from his teeth so his tongue could work.

"GREEEESSS-EEE?" I mimed the movement of his lips but let my tongue slop and flop freely.

"No. GRRRR-EASY." Mr. Dunn pressed his fingers into an O.K. symbol as he stretched out his syllables. "GR. EASY."

"GREESY. I said it. GREESY. What else you want?"

I refused to thumb through boring-ass baby books like *Shiloh* or *Maltida* or *Beezus and Ramona* during individual reading time. Instead, I slouched in the back of class reading the latest *Conan the Barbarian* I had dug out of my dead uncle's comic book collection. Those comics were musty and pulpy and dusty and bloody and lewd. Mutant dudes fisted tanks while masked women shrink-wrapped in body suits sauntered through fire like modern witches, color bleeding through grid panels, pages flaking grit on my fingertip.

Watching Conan dethrone emperors and deflower virgins satisfied me in a primal place deep in my guts where vestigial organs pumped Mesozoic-era secretions. Mr. Dunn tried confiscating my comics but quickly gave up once he realized I kept at least four more in my backpack. Demerits didn't matter. I used detentions for extra reading time.

I was sitting through detention, a burnt eraser smell giving me a headache, a great oak tapping the window like an impatient playmate, an ashy finger on page twelve of the *Conan* issue where our hero must kill a foreign king, when Mr. Dunn pulled a little yellow chair next to me, forced his middle-aged butt into that middle-school seat, and told me, "Avery, good buddy, you're smart—I'll give you that—but your head's thick as mutton. The homework just isn't getting done. It's a crying shame, but you're about ready to flunk out."

Mr. Dunn was close, too close. I kept my eyes on the comic. I didn't want to see my dumb, dopey face reflected in Mr. Dunn's eyes.

CLANG! Conan's mighty sword bounced off the king's enchanted breast plate. The king drew a scimitar, bejeweled and curved like an elephant's tusk.

"If you don't get better, your friends will move on without you," Mr. Dunn said. His stale coffee breath scrubbed the side of my face.

I turned away from him. I turned the comic's page.

SWIK! The foreign king swung back, his scimitar a white crescent in the desert sun. Conan—tanned and wild—ducked. The king's blade only trimmed his ink-black mane.

"Don't you care, buddy?"

SWIK! SWAK! SWIK! The king unleashed a flurry of slashes, but for all his bulk, Conan dodged and weaved smooth as a sidewinder.

"Avery, don't tell me you don't care at all. . . ."

SWAK! Stumbling back, the king's arm hung slack at his side. His sword dragged a line in the sand. His mouth was slanted in wordless surrender. Conan counterattacked.

"N'all, Mr. Dunn. I don't think I really do care at all. Sho'll don't."

SPLAK! The king's head flew off his spasming shoulders.

SINCE I WOULDN'T listen to reason, Mr. Dunn pinned my collar with a note for my parents. Kids avoided me for the rest of the day like

I had ringworms spiraling up my face. Mr. Dunn might as well have branded *DUMMY* on my neck—the sizzling, tender blisters would've hurt less. Every fifteen minutes, he checked the tape sealing the edges of the note to make sure I hadn't read it. He shouldn't have worried. I surely didn't want to see my stupidity described in his bold, blocky letters.

I wasn't going to let my family read that stupid letter either. They wouldn't understand, and worse, they'd get on my head. Yell would wallpaper my room with her honor roll certificates and mock me with a smug sneer. Mom would beat my ass off, hot glue it back on, and beat it off again. Grandma would oversee Mom's ass-whooping and tell her *Go'n, Cheryl. Snap your wrist into it. Hit him harder. He can take it. They don't break.* Granddad would snort cigarette smoke through his nose as he shook his head. Dad would disown me. Education was deathly important to him. He believed it was one of the few ways an upper-lower-class kid like me could snatch a key from a gatekeeper.

I thought about the gatekeepers as I moped in the corner of Fine Art. I ate gristly, salty slices of Lunchables ham, and read that issue of *Conan* where a cult of evil sorcerers employs wraiths to steal his soul.

The wraiths had black holes for faces, their eyes distant, dying stars. They wore cloaks that shifted around their skeletal frames like smoke, ruby rings on their spidery fingers, and necklaces strung with keys to treasure vaults. I imagined those wraiths resembled the gatekeepers Dad had warned me about.

Me and Dad were cleaning trash out of our backyard the first time he told me about them. Brown paper bags blended in with dead leaves. Tallboys littered creeping ivy like spent shell casings from an unbelievably big gun. A used condom, scummy and ominous as a molted snake skin, dangled off the branch of an evergreen shrub.

Dad told me *Gatekeepers hold all the keys, all of them.* He swept an arm at the vacant lot across the street where two ancient cars rotted like stumps of wood. *Gatekeepers hold the key to those Beamers zapping through traffic.* He swept his arm at the condemned house leaning at the end of the block. *Gatekeepers hold the keys to that big house on the hill.* He picked a twig off the ground and forked that condom off the evergreen bush. He flicked the putrid thing over our chain link fence into the alley. *Gatekeepers hold the key out of this goddamn place.*

MR. DUNN'S NOTE flapping on my breast pocket was a confirmation of the failure everybody figured I'd be. Once glitter set on glue-stick-lathered construction paper, and Fine Arts ended, I escaped the watchdogging Mr. Dunn, snuck into the service elevator, and rode up to the roof. I dug into my backpack through pages of attempted homework and tangy, powderized Smarties. I suffered the puke smell of rotten 7-11 egg salad sandwiches and found a bottle rocket. I stuck a few pieces of chewed gum on the note and wrapped it around the bottle rocket. I took a lighter out of the secret pocket I had paid Yell ten dollars to sew into my backpack. I lit the fuse, set my untied sneakers firmly in the gravel, and aimed that hissing bottle rocket at puffy, loping clouds. The bottle rocket whistled into the air and *POP-POPPED!* Sparks arced across the flat blue sky. Sulfur seethed in my head.

NONE OF MR. DUNN'S notes reached home. So the next week, he sent epic length letters to my house and laid siege to the answering machine. But collecting the mail was my chore, and I had resupplied my backpack with bottle rockets from a soggy box in the basement. Nobody listened to the answering machine anyway. Legions of creditors called from limbo, their nasally, droning voices eulogizing accounts long dead.

When Dad picked me and Yell up in the afternoons, Mr. Dunn stood on the curb, waving his arms wide as if megaton bombs were dropping. I hustled into the Taurus, kicking Yell's butt into the back seat as Dad shot back a dismissive wave and pulled off.

"How was school, Avery?" Dad would ask me.

"Great," I'd tell him.

"Great. I'm glad," he'd say and then he'd turn up the radio, smothering silence with pots and pans jazz.

As long as I kept destroying the notes, there was no way Mom or Dad would find out I was flunking. They never signed progress reports or attended parent-teacher conferences. Mom was always tired from her day job, her part-time job, and her part-time, part-time job. Dad was always tired from gambling during the night, working too-strange-to-be-true sales jobs during the day, and thinking of new excuses for commissions that never came in. His current venture was selling vending machines stocked with cheap, off-brand snacks like Kat-Kats, N & N's, and Thicker's Peanut and Nougat Style Treat Bar.

Besides, Mom and Dad thought my tenth-percentile state test scores combined with my ability to randomly ace history and science tests prophesied my hidden genius. Any 100 percent perfect score I could flash was never the product of diligent study. Really, I hated everything about tests.

My brain would lock down at the sight of blank lines and empty multiple-choice circles. I always scratched my head, hoping I might be able to dig into my scalp and free a few answers. Nothing bubbled out except for blood, clumping wet and dark under my fingernails like fresh dirt. So, I filled in the blanks without thinking, focusing more on creating dot patterns of GoBots, tough dogs, and middle fingers than scoring correct answers.

Soon my pencil would move automatically. As the smell of lead steamed hot in my nose, I remembered facts that must've soaked into my synapses while I thumbed textbooks and daydreamed during educational videos: modern birds evolved from raptors covered in downy plumage; Native Americans made bracelets out of cow bone; energy cannot be created or destroyed, only redirected into different forms; the sun will someday bloat into an angry red giant and devour the solar system; no storms, no blizzards trouble the Land of Milk and Honey.

The letters and calls finally stopped assaulting my house toward the end of the week. On Thursday morning, Mr. Dunn yanked me out of class during snack time, pinned another note on my collar, and told me, "I want you to know that the unadulterated truth will set you free."

"Nuh-uh. The truth can't set me free if I'm floating face-down in the Mississippi."

"I am only trying to help you."

"No. You're not. You're trying to get my dumb ass killed."

Mr. Dunn's cheeks reddened. I'm sure he wanted to slip a cyanide-dripping needle behind my ear and euthanize me like an errant kid in *The Giver*. Old dude didn't understand.

Sure, sometimes I could ace tests, but I failed just as many, and homework was one of the snarling, pterodactyl-winged, snake-tailed beasts stalking my dreams. I didn't know as much as I pretended to know. I didn't know why *He hurt him badly* was correct and *He hurt him bad* wasn't. Why astrology could help me pick winning lotto numbers while astronomy couldn't. Why if I divided four into sixty-four and ended up with a remainder of five, I must have done something dead wrong.

When I brought Dad a worksheet brutalized with scratch marks and rubbed raw with eraser, he liked to tell me *Avery, they want to see what you can do, not what I can do* and turn up the volume on whatever football game, hocking slurs when his team fumbled. What I could do academically was nothing worth saving. I thought Mr. Dunn had realized this fact by Friday.

He didn't pin a new note to my collar. He didn't slant his eyebrows into a disapproving *V*. He just let me be, let me have my petty victory in our eternal battle of wills. Flaunting my win, I openly reread the issue of *Conan* where our hero must kill an infernal harem of succubi with a sentient spear. Every third-grade boy and one fourth-grade girl huddled around me to giggle at all the bare, ink blot nipples and crude curves.

But on that afternoon, my victory revealed itself to be a shimmering illusion spun by Mr. Dunn's stealthy wizardry when I slid into the backseat of the Taurus next to Yell and saw a note—one of his notes—pinned to her collar.

I felt a rusty hook jerking out my innards, intestines swimming like mud-water eels. Yell's face was blotchy red with anger under the concealer Mom let her wear to camouflage throbbing whiteheads. I grabbed a pen and wrote demands on crumpled notebook paper. Me and Yell argued back and forth.

DESTROY that note?
I walked around looking like a fool all damn day, cuz of nobody but YOU!!!

Pretty Please? With sugar boogers?

NO! Why should I help a stone cold dummy?!

Just Don'T Snitch... You'll Kill me Dead.

A whole week passed before my life ended during a great game of after school soccer. The game was three on three at the playground. It was me, Jack Schleps, and "funky" Phil Landers, both of them blessed with wood blocks for feet, against Adam Jinks, Legs Pinker, and Paulie Weston, the best third-grade forward, defender, and goalie team. The score was tied, five-five. Jinks's Mom was bleating on her horn, but Jinks kept charging for that tiebreaker. He dribbled a neat *Z* around Jack, stutter stepped, eased the ball through Phil's legs, then charged me. Jinks flipped the ball into a rainbow over his head. Where other kids might have stumbled, I took my chance to strike.

BAM! I Tiger Knee'd the ball out of mid-air and landed on a wobbly settle. Legs threw a reckless, locomotive slide tackle that I easily hopped. I curved around him and banked the ball off the sandbox and back to myself just to show off. Buffalo-backed Paulie was the only thing between me and that last point. His specialty was rolling on the ground like a fool and snatching the ball from opposing feet with his long, sloth hands.

In the distance behind Paulie, I saw Dad pulling up to the curb.

Mr. Dunn was there like usual, but he wasn't flapping his arms or trying to jump on the hood of Dad's car. Mr. Dunn's posture was cool and confident. He worked the knot of his tie tighter.

Paulie was on his knees, hands out at his sides, a hockey goalie stance. The plan was to move in an *S* and chip the ball just over his shoulder, but I was too busy watching Dad. He stepped out of the car and shook hands with Mr. Dunn. HE SHOOK HANDS WITH MR. DUNN! My feet fell out of sync and the asphalt slipped under me. Paulie stretched out on his side and pawed the ball into his chubby arms.

Mr. Dunn pointed at me, his index finger like a laser gun. I felt a sizzle and a low, dense pop in the center of my skull. Dad nodded, his skinny arms folded. He and Mr. Dunn walked inside the school as best buddies, felicitous friends, co-conspirators.

I SKULKED OUTSIDE the fourth-grade classroom, snuffed at the doorjamb on all fours like a lonely dog, and then pressed my ear to the cold linoleum. I thought I might hear the distant thunder of hooves come to run me down, but instead I heard a peal of gentlemanly laughter. HAHAHAHAH!

After the laugher died, I tried to listen for Dad's voice, but his melodious salesman's murmur proved too slick and quick to hear. I could only make out Mr. Dunn's side of the conversation, his school teacher bass booming through the door.

Yes—yes, sir. You do pay good money and every bit of that . . . right. HAHAHAHA! *Well, my mother always told me there's smart, and then there's too smart—then there's just plain ornery.* HAHAHAHA!

Potential? What's potential worth if you just sit on it? HAHAHAHA! *Be that as it may, Mr. Colt, high test scores do not necessarily equate to success in the classroom. Or success in life. Right.* HAHAHAHA! *If you don't mind me asking, what's home life like?* HAHAHAHA! *Oh, I know he's not slow—never said he was slow, but—yes. Lazy. Yes. Lazy.*

HAHAHAHAHA!

Shame was cast-iron armor heavy on my shoulders and legs. If I was a crusader I would've exiled myself to the desert and let vultures peck my flesh, let the sun bleach my bones. If I was a Samurai, I could've seppuku'd and spilled my guts all over that giant cornucopia the second graders had built out of cardboard and plastic fruit. But I wasn't a crusader or a samurai—I was just a dumb kid.

I crouched by a bin of clothes for the homeless and snatched a dusty baseball cap. I put it on and yanked the brim down over my face. Some other kid's sweat was pungent in the cap's lining. I hoped the strange sweat might camouflage me, and Dad might mistake me for a straight A, all-star little leaguer, someone who wins little trophies and plaques. A kid who could competently swing Dad's youth league slugger without slipping on a rug.

My trick worked for a second. Dad came out of the classroom smiling with his lips and his cheeks, but not his eyes—no happiness in his eyes—and he looked right at me, but his eyes didn't focus. He couldn't acknowledge me just then. He turned back to Mr. Dunn.

"Say, you don't need a snack machine, do you?" Dad asked. "You could put it right there, next to the pop." Dad gave a grand sweep of his arm at the empty space next to the Coke machine. "We got this thing like a Twix, but without the cookie crunch. Real rich. Real smooth."

Mr. Dunn raised an eyebrow and told him, "Next you'll be trying to sell me Whatchamacallits without the what."

AH-HAAAAAA!
HAHAHAHA!

Dad laughed hard, the veins in his neck taut as wire. He shook his head, slapped his knee, but the last few *ha*'s out of his throat sounded more like low sobs than laughter. He exhaled and his whole body suddenly sagged like a punctured tire. I took that musty cap off and stood up straight, hopeful he might not be so mad. He looked at me, that fake smile fading off his face, and he said, "There's my main man. There he is. Man of the hour."

DAD DROVE NOWHERE and said nothing. No jazz wailed on the radio. Only car sounds broke the silence, ominous shudders from the transmission, junky squeaks from the rear axle, angry clicks every time Dad flicked the turn signal. Yell was gone on a field trip to Elephant Rock. I wished her a traitor's death. I prayed a horribly gaunt, long-fanged mountain lion would clamp the scruff of her neck and chuck her into a natural tomb of loose boulders.

Dread made the air heavy, my breaths shallow, my hands still. Mom would've already whooped me and then had me do fifty knuckle push-ups as I huffed *ONE! ONE-TWO!* No matter how many times I smashed my knuckles into the ground, they always felt soft as grapes and swelled tender for days. But Dad was different. He couldn't just hit me and be done. He had to jack around with my head to prove his point.

Me and Dad were halfway home when he jerked the car to a stop. He parked across the street from M.B. First Baptist Church. During the spring and summer, homeless folks ate stale bread and hot soup out of a tent in the parking lot. Those folks reminded me of the Morlocks, a group of X-Men mutants who resigned themselves to the sewers and shadows for fear of being judged for their deformities. When there was no soup and stale bread to be had at the church, these folks labored at Grandma and Granddad's general store, scrubbing grill racks, draining grease traps, taking Grandma's wrath for nothing more than a blue plate special and strong coffee. The houses around M.B. First Baptist were abandoned and decaying, urban blight spreading like the bacteria our class kept in a petri dish.

"Say, Avery, you see that man?" Dad asked. He pointed to a tall man wearing a two-sizes-too-small purple track suit. A spray of stringy black hair fell over his face. "See him? That raggedy looking man."

"Yeah," I said.

"You wanna be like him? When you grow up, I mean."

"No," I told him in an insulted squeak.

"What about that big gal over there—her—spilling that soup down her blouse. What's her name? Miss Marsh. That's right. You know she used to be a college professor—a college professor—before she came back here and lost her damn mind. Don't make a lick of sense, but that's what it is. You want to end up like her?"

"No."

"But what about. . . ." Dad tapped his fingers on his chin as he surveyed the parking lot. "What about Iron Joe? You see him, right? Pushing his good cart? What about him?"

Iron Joe was a local legend. He was known for pushing his shopping cart full of crushed soda cans, bushels of wires, and pipes through all elements—rain, heat, snow. He always walked shirtless and barefoot. He had skin dark and smooth as slate, a beard thicker than brambles, and a mouthful of bruised gums. He could be seen at any time of day or night scavenging soda cans from gutters, his cart *SQUEE-EAK, SQUEE-EAK, SQUEE-EAKING.*

"No, sir." I don't know why I called Dad sir. I must've been shook, for real.

"What you think them crushed pop cans are up to? About five cents a can? Ten cents?" Dad didn't want an answer, and I didn't want to give him one. "See those shoes in his cart?" I looked at Iron Joe's cart more closely and saw flattened shoes studding the metal and junk. Lord knows why they weren't on his feet. "I hear if he touches you, you turn to rust."

"Nuh-unh," I said.

"And I heard he eats kids just like you at night."

"But that man ain't got a tooth in his head."

"He swallows kids whole like a damn snake."

"He can't."

"He does, and boy, if you would listen, I'm trying to tell you there's a brand on your forehead. You can't see it yet, but it's there, and you need all the help you can get."

Dad unlocked the car doors. He shucked off his seatbelt and walked around to my side. He opened my door and got in my face.

"C'mon. You want to act like a chump, I'll set you out here with the rest of 'em."

I slouched and gripped my seatbelt until the rough edges bit into my hands.

"C'mon. They're all waiting," Dad said.

He yanked at my arm. I ripped at his dress shirt and tore off a button. His backhand was automatic. I could see *I'm sorry* in his eyes before his hand landed. The blow felt like hard thunder in my head. Star-shine bloomed behind my eyes. Warmth gushed out of my nose. The taste of iron was raw in the back of my throat.

"Shit!" Dad said. "Shit! Shit!" He scanned the street for witnesses. Scarecrow smirked and gulped his soup. Dad looked back at me, looked down at my shoes. He fiddled with the double-knot on my sneaker. "Now why'd you go and do that? Why'd you. . . ."

I couldn't tell if he was talking to me or himself. He laid a hesitant hand on my cheek. He snatched a handful of napkins out of the glove box and ripped them up. He pushed my head back and plugged my nostrils with the coarse napkin paper.

"Oh-boy," was all he could say. "Boy, boy, boy, boy."

DAD STOPPED AT a Crown Mart down the street. He put two dollars in my hand and told me, "Go on and get yourself a slushie." Then he put a ten into my hand and told me, "You know what, get yourself some Funyuns too." He reached into his pocket again, but I guess there was nothing else there. "But hey, little man," this was the first time he looked me in the face since he slapped the living mess out of me, "fix your face too."

I watched him walk off. Once he was out of sight, I flipped down the sun visor and opened the vanity mirror. The middle of my face was a black and red scab under the vanity mirror's copperish light. I spit into a napkin and wiped away the crusted blood from my nose like Mom would do. Inside the Crown Mart, I grabbed two bags of Funyuns, a Slim-Jim, a Hershey's bar, and one of those Ring-Pops I never really liked—Dad wasn't getting a penny of change back.

Dad got the bathroom key from the cashier, a ropey woman wearing a sheer wave cap over her low fade. He tried joking with her, asking if she might need a snack machine, maybe outside right next to that air hose. But she just kept thumbing through an *XXL* magazine, pretending not to hear him through the bulletproof glass.

"Back in a flash," Dad said as he yanked the bathroom door open.

I poured a cola slushie and marveled at how it perfectly corkscrewed into my too-big-for-god slushie cup. I stole a few slurps from under the spigot. The cold cut through my teeth in the best way.

I pushed my goodstuff on the counter by the register and dropped Dad's cash into the metal box below. I pocketed the quarters the cashier returned and started bagging everything up when I noticed her staring at me like *damn, what happened to you?*

"It's all this dry weather," I tried to tell her, but all that came out was, "Id albd dit dry webber."

The cashier just shrugged and went back to her *XXL*. Bizzy Bone was on the cover, mean-mugging hard.

Dad grunted in the bathroom, pushing out last night's pot roast. I walked out to the car by myself and took a squeegee to the bird shit on the car's windshield, hoping I could get an early start on my work toward redemption.

Premonitions of dinner that night played in my head: Before we eat, Dad breaks the bad news to Mom in the bedroom. Furniture slams and Mom's voice becomes a low roar. Dad says *I already set him straight, so be easy, okay?* We all chew our Shake and Bake chicken in the kind of silence that creeps along the floor like a chill vapor. Dad doesn't look at me. Mom doesn't look at me. Yell doesn't look at me, a smirk slashing her face. I try to leave the table, but Mom snatches my hand, looks up from her plate and says, *Avery, all I know is, you have got to do better. Now get down and give me twenty. Don't play with me—don't think I won't beat that ass.*

The taste of cola slushie turned stale in my mouth. I decided exile would be better than pain and humiliation. On the back of the Crown Mart receipt I wrote:

> Dear Family,
> Sorry I Am
> A failure.
> Sincerely,
> Avery Robert
> Colt

I laid the letter on the car's hood and admired the flow of my penmanship, the arch of my A's and the expert loops of my O's. I chugged slushie until my head felt like a cracking glacier and left the rest of that goodstuff on the pavement for squirrels to ravage. I tied my shoes tight, grabbed my backpack, ran.

*

I KEPT RUNNING until everything blurred into a stain. Gang-bangers in bright blue shared cigarillos and swigs of beer; A pack of saber-toothed dogs head-butted an unfinished wooden fence; A great old lady spiked a trowel in her flower bed, stood, cracked her back, and cried out; A hustler popped dust out of a pair of bootleg Tommy Hilfiger jeans; Cats yowled like colicky babies; Policemen stuffed mustaches with greasy St. Paul sandwiches; Little kids played tag, raced after me like I was it.

The horizon hacked the sun in half by the time I stopped running. Every lateral muscle on my right side was twisting into stone. Adrenaline thrummed in my head. Sweat salted my lips.

I was back by M.B. First Baptist. Dusk light pierced stained glass windows. Pigeons fought over bread left in the parking lot, banged their beaks like swords. For a hot minute, I savored the burnt caramel taste of a successful escape and bellowed my own gentleman-ly laughter *HAHAHAHAHAHAHA*! Then I heard *SQUEE-EAK* . . . *SQUEE-EAK* . . . *SQUEE-EAK* . . . high and tinny on the wind.

Dad might've lost me, but Iron Joe had picked up my trail. If I didn't move quickly, he'd capture me, swallow me whole, add my shoes to his collection. I cut into an alley between rows of abandoned houses.

The last few shadows of the day laced into oily fingers. Claustrophobia was a hand at my throat. There was one more *SQUEE-EAK* behind me. I turned. A ragged silhouette staggered toward me from the other end of the alley.

I took no chances. I dashed into the nearest abandoned house, hurdled rotting wooden steps in twos. On the porch there was a small shrine, stuffed animals wreathed in plastic flowers all huddled around a cross. Odd comfort settled in my chest. If evil lived there, a plush offering had already been made.

The house felt peopled. A presence lived in the peeling walls, crawled under floorboards. The staircase in front of me was crushed under debris, plaster flaked like dead skin. Wood paneling warped like gnarly toenails. In the living room a ladder rose through a hole in the ceiling. I kicked the ladder. It rattled but held steady enough.

I climbed up to the second floor and found a room empty except for a folded bed sheet, a soiled pillow, and a shattered mirror. A million me's stared out from the broken shards. Glass crunched under my sneakers.

The adrenaline finally cooled thick and viscous in my blood. I smoothed the bed sheet out on the floor and sat down, propping the pillow in the dewy small of my back. I lay back against the wall underneath a windowless window frame and imagined myself to be a rebel prince hiding out in crumbling castle ramparts.

My kingdom had long ago been conquered by an empire, their war machines brawling, flat hoofed, lethargic behemoths shucking jewelry off my people's wrists and necks, the red coral, the ivory, leaving only buttery pyrite in stunned, gawking mouths. Starting a revolution was an elephantine task for a dumb, flunkie kid. But I was amassing quick, bright swords in my mind, ballistics in my heart.

HAHAHAHA! Mean laughter rumbled downstairs, rough and saw-bladed. Invaders had infiltrated my castle. I couldn't tell if they were mercenaries sent by Mr. Dunn, Iron Joe's minions, or agents of the Gatekeepers. I crawled over to the hole by the ladder and scouted them out. Two men and one woman composed the invading party. One man had an onion bulb head. The other man had a cast-iron pot belly. The woman's face was wrinkled as a rhino's shin, but her arms were toned and slender, girlish. They shared pints of clear liquor, and Onion Head said a sentence that sounded like *fuck-fuck-fuck-ole'-bitch-ass-fuck,* making the other two guffaw.

"You sho'll right," Rhino Shin hollered. "Ain't nothing but punks round here, but like I been saying, you could kill yourself worrying about what this or that nigga think."

Those invaders had no venom tipped knives sheathed on their hips, so I figured they weren't assassins. Maybe they were refugees fleeing from a hundred-year war. But I wasn't completely sure. I kept watch for an ambush.

The last touches of dusk light flattened to nothing. Bluish dark spread and then the moon lumbered out, full and silver, crinkled like chewed foil. Moonlight shot through every crack in that ruined house, vaporizing the dark. A lighter *FLIK–FLIKED* and flame leapt from a hand downstairs. Sour smoke rose. A smell like boiling Windex slithered through my lungs.

The moonlight cut Pot Belly's face into bands as he wheezed and wrestled the ladder. He was coming up. He was going to see me and collect my head for his ransom. The adrenaline returned, a grinding whine in my ears.

Pot Belly's feet banged up the ladder. The ladder shivered. I shivered. I jumped up, fumbled through my backpack, snatched out a clump of damp bottle rockets. *FLIK-FLIK!* My little lighter fizzled sparks but couldn't throw flame. The ladder shivered and banged. He was coming up, ready to saw through the gristle in my neck. *FLIK-FLIK! FLIK-FLIK! FLIK-WOOSH!*

Fire braided the bottle rocket's fuse. I aimed. The ladder shivered and banged. Pot Belly was almost up. His head crowned through the hole in the floor, a skull floating up out of Tartarus. Sparks seared my knuckles. He saw me, a flabby little hellion. Fire hissed at my fingertips. He started to holler, "Now what in the hell—" *FWOOM!* The bottle rocket shot, screamed, exploded—*POP-POP!*

Steel-blue sparks pinwheeled off his forehead. He hollered and fell back down the hole. Dust shook from the ceiling above me. Onion Head groused *fuck-fuck-fuck-ole'-bitch-ass-fuck!*

I extended out the window frame. Peaks of broken glass sliced the webbing between my fingers. I hooked my ankles behind the storm gutter, squeezed it between my thighs, dug my palms into the grooves, and Spider-Manned my way down. Jagged metal scraped my hands. I let go and fell into a thicket of weeds and fast food wrappers. I sprang to my feet like a Super-Ball. No bones felt broken. I was alive and whole, but my house key was gone. I looked up and saw it hanging from a nail jutting off the windowsill. Something thin and black whipped through the air above me. White bone shone in moonlight.

STREETLIGHTS BLINKED DROWSILY, hard copper eyes watching me stumble through scattered ruins. I was halfway home. My knees knocked and seized like dull gears. Tattered flaps of skin peeled off my shredded hands. I was exhausted and ready to admit my absolute failure at being worthy.

"Avery!" A shrill voice called my name. "Avery!" the voice called again. I squinted into the distance, afraid that I might see a battalion of Gatekeepers swooping down on me, thick and consuming as a storm cloud, but I saw something much stranger.

Mom drove Dad's car down the street at a steady crawl, her head out the window, shouting my name. Her earrings caught the streetlight and winked. Yell was in the backseat, dutifully shining a flashlight into murky side streets, rolling her eyes every time she didn't see my nappy hide. Dad jogged alongside the car like he was taking last place in a long marathon. Streetlights buzzed on and off as my family trudged forward, leaving them in alternate shades of shadow and dim light. They looked beaten and miserable in their designer clothes.

I was afraid they'd reject me, surrender me to wraiths who'd make necklaces out of my tongue and teeth, leave me in the street to gulp soup and scrounge gutters for tin with Iron Joe and the Morlocks, let Mr. Dunn club me with dictionaries until I was nothing but bland, pink mush. But I had survived one day by my own wit. For once, my knuckles felt strong, hard as rock. I was ready for punishment. I stepped out into the street, waved my arms high, and hollered.

HEY!

BAD BEAT

DAD PLAYED ME for a fool. He claimed I was the descendant of Egyptian caliphs, that treasure lived inside me. I'd fall asleep with visions of rubies flowing through my blood, microscopic corpuscles glittering, ventricles pumping gemstones by the millions. I'd imagine my bones as African ivory, my skin as burnished brass, my spine as iron harnessed from the heart of mountains. Every part of me was precious, valuable, and more than worthy—that's the kind of bullshit Dad told me before he'd disappear for days and try to win that bad beat. *You can be on your last two dollars and still be rich* he'd say. *Don't forget that.*

I wish I knew what kind of bullshit he told Yell. He'd whisper in her ear, and she'd resist him, her body coiled tight and trembling, hands scrunched into delicate fists, gnashing her tongue. At thirteen years old, she should've been too wise for his bullshit. But late at night, after Dad was long gone, and Mom had called every last riverboat casino bobbing in Mississippi sludge (*Yes, hello, is a Richard Colt there? Yes. Poker table—who am I? I'm his wife. Yes. Okay. No. Okay. I'll hold*), Yell would heap candy necklaces around her chicken neck, stand on her tiptoes, and announce, "By holiest decree of the Nile and all earthly kingdoms, thou shalt address me as QUEEN!"

The bullshit Dad laid on Mom was more nuanced, not so outlandish. He sold some of his riverboat excursions as date nights. Mom fashioned herself like a backup singer in a classic R&B group, hot curling her hair into copper spangles, snapping on a pearl necklace, wobbling in too-high heels, smoothing clingy dresses over her thighs, glossing her nails like Red Hots, exposing every tender keloid on her chest.

When they came back home with purse and pockets fatally wounded, Dad would sit Mom on the porch steps and tell her about Easy Street, a mythical land where stone mansions hulked, and Range Rovers cruised the streets, behemoths in chrome.

Those date nights devolved into Dad going out by himself and bringing home dinner at three in the morning, brown bags heavy with gristly hot wings, mealy cheeseburgers, and soggy fries bought with his comp card.

He'd stagger back in the house, looking beat up, a wilted peacock feather in his bowler hat, bunches of wrinkles in his leisure suit. But he still had the nerve to blow velvety plumes of cigarette smoke and smile, a man satisfied with his hard labor.

When Mom got on his head about wasting the money she had made grinding out double shifts at Dillards, he'd sigh like the wind was crushed out of him and say *Honey, I don't know what to tell you. I'm not doing this for my health.*

Soon, he lost his job selling vending machines because of gambling binges. Whether he quit or got fired was a carnal mystery. Every day, he slept deeply like a junkie, sunlight blazing on his bloated face. Every night, he jaunted out that door as if he had stolen the key to infinite recess.

When Dad was out hustling, I'd creep into the lounge where he kept his sports trophies. Figurines of quarterbacks and track stars frozen in mid-stride guarded that sacred space. Their brows creased as I entered unbidden and sniffed the air for his scent like a lonely dog. I'd sink into his leather recliner and read the musty, crumbling comics my dead uncle had left in the attic.

Bizarre scenes filled those yellowed pages. Psionic mind beams ripped black holes in the fabric of time and space. Barbarians gutted ruthless warlords. Cyborgs defused atomic bombs. I'd clap the comics shut and fantasize that an unforeseen catastrophe held Dad captive, that he was caught in the tentacles of a shovel-headed kraken, its beak crushing the boat's boiler, poker chips, cards, and cash falling into murky water.

NOW MOM DIDN'T play when it came to taking care of the house. If you left bacon grease in the microwave, nasty dish water in the sink, garbage overflowing out of the trash can, she was getting that ass. Me and Yell turned punishments into gross competitions. We used to compare welts from belts, cuts from switches. We'd see who could stand one-legged in the corner for the longest, who could buck the most knuckle pushups on that hardwood floor, splinters jutting from the webbing between our fingers.

Mom did us like that, but said nothing to Dad, even though he did squat. Months passed after he lost his job, and soon, he started treating bills like suggestions, not contracts or promises. Utilities in our half of the house became willful, lazy. Lights blinked off at their leisure. The water heater stopped clanging and rumbling, leaving cold free to bully hallways in winter. The phone bleated robotic *"I'm sorry"s* when numbers were dialed. Mom refused to beg Grandma and Granddad for help. They'd just snort real mean, shake their heads.

So Mom wore heavier makeup, slashed her lips red, and picked up weekend shifts, but said nothing to him. Grandma told her *That man ain't no good, Cheryl. You better get it together and find you a new one.* Granddad threatened to put a boot in Dad's ass and put him to work cleaning counter tops and grease traps at the corner store. Mom still said nothing to him. But after losing grocery money on a rash of terrible bluffing one night, he returned home with enough nerve to beg Mom for her emergency stash. Finally she said something to him.

"Lose. That's all you ever do, Richard," she confronted Dad, curses bunched in her jaw. It was about four-something in the morning, and a full moon was melting into blue-black sky like a dot of candy on God's tongue. A few stubborn, glassy stars held their orbits, spiteful of dawn. Me and Yell poked holes in the screen door as Mom cleaved Dad with axe-headed truths.

"Then you wanna come to me, begging, telling me we can have this, we can do that, and every motherfucking time I'm fool enough to follow you. Every motherfucking time. But I say NO just once. Just once, and you throw a fit like I owe you something." She folded her arms over her long t-shirt, the one with the ugly Siamese cat on the front. Her biceps flexed. "You got to pay the cost to be the boss, and baby, I'm telling you, them IOUs don't cut it."

Dad didn't fuss or cuss back. He just nodded coolly and nonchalantly chugged cigarette smoke as if Mom was simply asking his opinion about what flowers to plant in the yard and not punting his balls high over roofs. He waved his cigarette and said, "I'll win it all back, easy." He cheesed hard, trying to be debonair and reassuring. His smiles were dazzling but strained like an old theater marquee, bulbs overworked and about to blow.

Mom shook her head violently and said, "I don't want to hear it."

"With interest. Double or nothing."

"Kick that shit elsewhere, man."

"You know I will. I just need—"

"What you need is a good ass-whooping. Now go on and just leave, Richard. Leave, before I find the strength."

Dad's shroud of cool cracked for a hot second. He scowled as if offended by a bad smell. Cords in his neck tightened. But then that second passed, his shoulders slackened, and he shrugged. He stubbed his cigarette on the porch ledge and stretched his arms to the sky like a kid bored in PE class. He turned to me and Yell for the first time that night, told us, "Wish me luck, y'all," and bounded down the steps to his Taurus.

Dad's Taurus grunted and hacked before grinding into a rough, rocking idle. That stupid hooptie was in the shop every week. Even though mechanics blamed breakdowns on hoses and dog-toothed gears, I knew the problem was gremlins—just had to be gremlins. I used my Batman binoculars to perform surveillance this one time, and I saw sparks popping, webbed claws fidgeting under the car, heard the high tinkle of bolts falling. Dad waved goodbye as the Taurus leaked fluid and loped away, a miserable, wounded thing.

Mom turned on me next. She snatched Yell out of the way, thumped me against the wall, and told me through clenched teeth,

"Avery, I have money in this house. If that man comes back here when I'm gone, don't you dare let him in. I don't give a single, sorry fuck if he's bleeding, dying, spilling his goddamn guts—you do not let him in. You hear me? Do not."

I nodded a stiff *yes ma'am.*

WITH MOM WORKING a double at Dillards, Granddad and Grandma tending the corner store, and Yell running the streets, guarding the house was on my narrow shoulders. I stealthed into Dad's lounge, stole an old slugger, contracted stray cats to patrol the gangway, and secured a perimeter around the front porch. I scattered tacks on the stone steps, slicked the porch with three-day-old fish grease. But none of my fortifications mattered. Dad didn't come through the front door.

I was practicing thrusts and parries with the slugger when I heard thudding and crashing from inside the house. I sheathed the slugger in a belt loop, banged through the screen door, ran up the steps, and found Dad thrashing the living room. He kicked over ottomans, clawed couch and recliner cushions, battered closet shelves, all while shouting *LOUSY BITCH!* and *BULLSHIT! BULLSHIT!* with nasty, thorned joy. I watched him quietly, sweaty hand on that slugger, waiting for that rage to drain.

He tore a curtain off its rod just to be ornery and flopped down on the couch, his bony butt sinking into the flimsy box springs. He picked his nails and pouted—there was nothing so disturbing as seeing a full-grown man seriously pout. As he snatched a fresh cigarette out of his breast pocket, he paused, glaring at a hole slit in the couch's fabric. Revelation smoothed stress lines in his forehead. He punched a greedy fist through that hole and rejoiced.

"Ha-ha! Got ya!" he trumpeted, his smile brilliant, a mess of bills wrinkled between his knuckles. Then he noticed me. That cheap smile peeled right off like a dirty sticker. His whole body crumpled with uncontested embarrassment. He pinched creases out of his sleeve, offered a weak, "Hey-hey, buddy," and broke for the back door.

I leapt in front of him, drew the slugger—*SWIK! SWAK!*—and barked, "You can't go!"

Dad sighed and jammed that cigarette in the corner of his mouth. "Avery, would you please cut the bullshit."

I leveled the slugger and pressed forward—*SWAK! SWAK!* "Mom said you're not allowed in the house."

"Oh, is that right? She made you man of the house, hunh?"

"Right," I said. "That's right."

"So you the man of the house and don't know to lock a back door, keep some eyeballs in the back of your head." He lit that cigarette and pocketed the money so quickly, I thought it was a magic trick, "Mm . . . I'm sorry to say, my friend, but you're not off to a great start."

"Whatever."

"Whatever," he mocked me. "Whatever," he sighed. "Now will you please move?"

I didn't move. I had a brief fantasy of beating him with that bat, ripping his snazzy leisure suit to tatters, and stomping on his hands until he gave back every last dollar. But I couldn't beat down a grown man, not with all the muscle definition of a steamed yam. I lowered that slugger and thought of a fair compromise. "I can let you go . . . under one condition."

"What in the world do you want out of me?"

"Not a whole lot. Just take me with you."

"Oh-no, Avery. No, no, no, no, no. No."

"I just wanna see what it's like."

"It's none of your business."

"I won't be a problem at all. Promise."

"Boy, I bet you could sell a bucket of hot coals to the devil himself, talk a good church lady out her drawers." Dad clapped his hands on my shoulders and leaned into me. Even though we were fighting, I relaxed at his touch. A mild sedative must have seeped from his fingertips. "But, lemme tell you something—"

Dad spat a rank miasma of cigarette smoke and sour vodka breath in my face, and before I could rub that acrid burn out of my eyes, he swept my ankles and wrenched me to the floor. My skull banged off hardwood, my teeth clacked violently, jagged stones swelled in my temples.

Dad's knockoff gators thumped down the steps and out the side door, and I knew better than to chase, but curiosity was louder than the chimes breaking in my head. If my ribcage was perfect ivory, my heart a massive ruby; If Yell harbored the immortal soul of an Egyptian queen; If Mom was heiress to Easy Street fortunes, then what was so wondrous, magnificent, goddamn irresistible about some poker room lodged in the stinking guts of a glitzed up, sludge-farting steamer?

Groaning, I staggered to my feet and scrambled out after him. My head felt stale. Cracked floorboards on the back porch wobbled under my feet. The noon sun attacked me with salvos of cruel light.

Dad's Taurus stalled out in the alley, stressed engine squealing protest, belching oily fumes. There was an abrupt, bombastic *POP! POP! POP*ing followed by *CLINK-CLINK!* and Dad fumbled out of the Taurus then slammed the car door once, twice for emphasis. He saw me, grimaced, and jabbed a finger at me through the air so hard I could feel his nail in my sternum. "Stay in your place."

I should have listened, but I dogged him all the way to the bus stop instead.

"Avery, I'm going to tell you one last time—Go home."

I jangled change in my pocket. "Look, I have enough to get on the bus."

"Why do you have to be so goddamn worrisome?"

I counted the change in my palm. "Bus fare's a dollar, right?

"Thorn in my side, boy. Bunion on my big toe—just worrisome as I-don't-know-what."

"Dang. Ten cents short." I saw a few flattened pennies and nickels glinting in the gutter. "Never mind—got it."

"Avery."

I fought off visions of mutant, sawtoothed rats equipped with toxic venom sacs as I scrounged change from the gutter.

"Avery, you don't wanna go down there with me. It's not kid stuff—ain't nothing nice. I am telling you. Nothing nice."

I thrust a handful of scum-coated coins up at him. "See? Got it. No problem."

Dad gently laid a hand on my shoulder and said, "Son—"

I shrugged his hand away, so he couldn't dump me again.

That lazy charm he relied on melted. He slowly collapsed into a deep sulk as if his spine had been jerked out with pliers. "Son, lemme try again. I can't tell you what kind of hold that place has over you. I can't tell you what it is, but I can tell you what it feels like. Smoke and whispers soak up hours, them free drinks make your brain nothing but a wet sponge, your tongue sticks to the roof of your mouth like salt water taffy, and you bet and bet until your pockets are bone dry, then you bet some more—and for what? I don't know, but ain't that ugly?"

I ignored the plea in his voice and said, "Hey, the bus is coming."

"Did you listen to a word I just said? Sometimes I don't know who in the world raised you. I'm telling you it's awful, nothing nice at all. Nothing but a bunch of fools scrapping over gizzards and bones."

ONCE ME AND Dad boarded the bus, it wouldn't be long before I saw a bit of that ugliness. The bus was a flea market pumped up on hydraulics, staffed with all manners of hustlers. In the front row of seats, a woman with long black and orange dreadlocks sold bootleg DVDs and packages of socks. "I got that new-new, three for ten, five for fifteen, and get you a clean pair of socks too," she cried. "You hear me? Get them stank rags off your feet."

In the middle row of seats there was a greasy dude in a frumpy suit selling mismatched kitchen knives out of a briefcase. He held up and described each knife. "Carving knife . . . nine and a half inches . . . pure stainless steel . . . chef's knife . . . ten inches . . . triple riveted . . . one-hundred-and-twenty percent premium carbonite." In the back row of seats, an old man invited passengers to play a shell game.

"Come to bat and get 'em skinny pockets fat!" the old man hollered as he flicked bottle caps into tight circles. Clockwise. Counter clockwise. Clockwise again. He shuffled three bottle caps on top of an employment guide, flashing a pinto bean here and there, his fingers intelligent, articulate machines concealing motives all their own. "Y'all don't be scary! Place a bet, we'll be set! Throw down five, this game come alive!"

Those hokey, taunting rhymes lodged sparkling hooks in my soft, jelly-head, fascinating me, willing me to study the dizzying swoop and spiral of those bottle caps as if I could discover coded rhythms and claim the pot. I couldn't buy in with just a stick of Juicy Fruit cocooned in pocket lint. Passengers pulled musty, crumpled dollars from sneakers and bras, crowded that old man, and laid cash at his feet, whooping after winning once or twice, cursing as losses stung methodically.

Not one of the passengers dropping cash was a jewel-laden big-shot, no bright wrists plated in platinum, no squat necks laced in gold. N'all. They were just regular folks who had bad haircuts, bad teeth, and thrift store clothes on their backs, all of them wishing Lady Luck might appear by their side, trap that bean between her fingernails.

The shell game was a lusterless vortex spinning under that old man's hands, sucking up money and whatever else passengers dared to bet. Shuffle. Shuffle. Shuffle. Stop. Shuffle. Stop. Left. Right. Middle. Choose. They bet and lost dollars, coins. Shuffle. Stop. Shuffle. Stop. Left. Right. Middle. Choose. They bet and lost anklets, glass baubles. Shuffle. Shuffle. Stop. Shuffle. Stop. Left. Right. Middle. Choose. They bet and lost cans of potted meat, bags of synthetic hair.

Those sparkling hooks of fascination dislodged from my brain with a wet, squelching pop. That old man wasn't running game. N'all. He was selling cheap, bargain-bin hope to the desperate. A stupid kid like me could see that, but somehow, Dad couldn't.

Dad told me, "See him? See this man working? You better see him, because he sure sees us. I bet he could tell your future from a pile of chicken bones, make a mink coat out of rat hide. Shoot, I bet he'd snatch the damn moon out the sky and sell it to you for twenty-five cents. Yeah, buddy—but you know what? I got his number all day. Got him like a bad cold. Like how them thugs say: Game recognize game, and I got him. Now watch me." Dad tossed five dollars on the floor and called, "Right here!"

"Step right up, go'n lay it down!" that old man announced, withered fingers shuffling the bottle caps. Dad straightened his bowler, hunkered in front of the shell game, looked back at me, and nodded. His carefully acted front of boyish confidence had finally gassed out, leaving behind weary, skeletal frustration. He had to have known the old man would take everything valuable to him, leech the ivory from his bones, shave the brass off his back, split open his breast, steal fractured ruby from his heart. Dad still had enough nerve to hunker down, wink, and play the game.

MOST VALUABLE PLAYER

I HADN'T SET a foot in Dad's lounge for months after he left. Icy moonlight sliced through venetian blinds and transmuted his junk into supernatural relics: blues records became dusty, cracked obsidian mirrors; shamanic potions bubbled inside cologne bottles. I slapped the light switch on, a bare bulb oozed amber, and I half-expected, half-hoped I might find his mummified corpse sagging in a recliner, sulfuric swamp moss burning ghoulish gray on his scalp, jewel beetles crawling from between shriveled lips. There was no grotesquerie waiting for me, just his trophies lined up and useful as dead idols.

Whenever Mom cussed the cool out of his walk, Dad barricaded himself in that lounge and power cleaned every trophy he had, including the small, dinky ones he kept boxed in the closet. I'd get a toothbrush and help, full-strength ammonia fumes scorching my airways so raw it felt like I was breathing mustard gas. My brains were always reduced to rotten pumpkin guts by the time we'd finish, but at least those trophies shined, figurines bolting through end zones, tracers zipping behind cleated strides.

After reorganizing each trophy according to sport, year, and honor, Dad would lazily swing the slugger he won in a youth league home run derby and brag on his prowess. *Oh yeah, I was something else back in the day, waaaaaay back in the day. Boy, I had the legs of a goddamn jackrabbit, gunpowder in my arms. Yessir, yessir. I had high-powered diesel pumping through my blood, talked trash like I ate breakfast at the junk yard. College scouts love that kind of confidence, ya' dig? Wouldn't have landed that good track scholarship without it. Truthfully, who wants to back some coward?*

Dad would smash imaginary pop flies and cluck as they sailed nowhere. *Oh yeah, I was a real dynamo. If I had it my way, I would've kept right on chugging.* Then he'd grimace, lean on that youth league slugger like it was a cane, and recite that awful litany of injuries that ended his athletic career. Multiple forearm and wrist fractures. A left knee stripped bald of cartilage. Too many concussions to remember. He even had mint-condition x-rays of those screws in his shoulder blade, his bones white and ghastly, ectoplasm on black film.

Next came ritualistic deliberation as he fabricated straight razors out of nostalgia and opened new wounds, telling me what could've been, should've been. *You know I had a honest shot at the Olympics? Pulled my damn hamstring during qualifiers for that 200-meter sprint. I should have stuck with football, got lumped up enough for it. Half these turkeys ain't worth a shit, and they pull down millions—millions—can you believe that?* He'd grimace again, a long silence would yawn, and then he'd look at me with this cautious hope. He'd say *Now, Avery, son, have I ever taught you how to swing* or *throw* or *punt* or *dribble?*

I'd answer, *probably not,* and then right there on that carpet, he'd drop that slugger and give me hasty lessons over three-point stances, tight spirals, and sliders. I'd try to follow his pantomimes and instructions, *snap your wrist, follow through, but don't go all herky-jerky. Bend those knees, turn to your right, no, your other right—I said your right. Dude, you are just killing me. Killing me dead, dumb, and stupid.*

I tried to follow him, but he moved too quickly, wrongly assuming his movements would naturally become my movements, that we were psychically connected by some genetic muscle memory. Once one of those awkward lessons was over, both of our faces would shine with sweat as we tried not to breathe hard in front of each other. He'd wave me off, chuckle, and go right back to bragging.

Boy, what I wouldn't give to be eighteen and out on the field, any field, again. Oooo-wee, I'd give a cool drink of water in Hell. Shoot, I'd sell Moses down the river. What I wouldn't give, boy. I had a pitch that'd put a comet to shame, a quarterback sneak nobody could crack.

Now alone in Dad's lounge, admiration and envy crossed swords inside my chest. I know he loved me, but his kind of love was a conditional, selfish creature that consumed hearts and longed for the next kill. I know he liked the admiration of a cheering crowd, the warmth of strange faces caught in his thrall. Me and my folks were short on throats and lungs. Our chorus could only crow so loud.

I felt a phantom touch on my shoulders as I hefted his slugger. That genetic muscle memory had been released. Those motions felt natural this time. My swings felt smooth and dangerous. I jogged to the backyard and practiced my batting on crushed soda cans. I missed the first few times, but eventually found a rhythm and connected, sending them scudding across asphalt and cobblestones. Once the soda cans were spent, I started in on those trophies and medals. I set the big trophies with heavy bases on the porch and pulverized them into splinters, screws, and cracked marble. Those dumb little figurines snapped off their pillars and littered the tall grass. His track medals flew furthest—*PING! PING!*—fading deep in a sky of dim stars.

PART II

GARDEN OF FIRE AND BLOOD

NOTHING BUT JUNK bloomed in that abandoned lot behind the corner store. Snarls of copper wire wrestled creeping ivy. Shattered glass glinted under lazy, wilting dandelions. Red bricks studded the dirt like toadstools. That lot would likely yield more bottle caps than green beans—even a blind man could see that—but Grandma thought she could punch seeds into the earth and bully out a garden, fat tomatoes hanging low, waxy peppers shining, buttercups popping, all lush and good smelling.

Now Granddad would've called Grandma a damned pig-headed fool if that stroke hadn't hit so hard and left him laid out in bed, arms and legs twisted like poisoned roots, craggy head sinking into over-fluffed pillows, red and yellow gunk oozing out the side of his mouth every time he coughed. I swear I heard junk rattling in his lungs too, bent nails and bolts.

Granddad was plain useless, a lump of petrified wood. Without him there to talk some good sense, Grandma worked the hairy, stanking dog ass out of me all summer, as if my sweat might nurture a bountiful New Eden.

Grandma barked, *Avery, pull up them weeds!* And I was throttling stubborn brambles out of the ground with no gloves, tough, green thorns tearing pink gashes in my knuckles. *Avery, cut down them branches!* I was shimmying up horse apple trees, chopping limbs with a wobbly machete—*THWACK! THWACK! THWACK!*—impacts rattling my teeth loose. I worked myself dumb as a dead stump. Scabs the size of wood beetles swarmed up and down my shins. Blisters lurched across my palms like slugs. I had never felt so useful. I was fourteen, and it felt good testing unfamiliar strength. After a few weeks of my strongest efforts, that abandoned lot was still full of weeds and wreckage. Of course, Grandma blamed the lack of progress on my pure laziness.

I was hoisting and stacking goliath cinder blocks to make a raised planting bed like that one Grandma had seen in *Better Homes and Gardens* when she shook her head and said, "Boy, I swear I've known canned Spam with more backbone than you." She leaned forward in her chair, shoulders hunched like a boxer. "You got no heart, no smarts, no strength—tell me, boy, what good is you?"

I had no answer.

I don't know why, but Grandma's insults always clung to me like science fiction leeches, drooling corrosive bile, chewing through soft spots in my head. Mean comebacks bunched in my jaw, but I didn't have the nerve to spit them. I hefted another cinder block. Grandma kept right on, telling me, "And you had better not be over there setting up my blocks all wrong, acting like a goddamn mongoloid."

The understood *or I will beat you deaf, dumb, and blind* was a hoarse whisper cutting through my hypothalamus, making my fight or flight switch jerk like an overworked arcade stick. All my life, Grandma had slashed axioms of moral decency and respect in my back with dog wood switches, old, burnt-out extension cords. It didn't matter that aggressive puberty was spoiling me with new biceps, height, and scrubby chest hair. She had implanted hard nodes of fear so close to the bone I could never cut them out.

"You hear me, boy? I said do it right."

The cinder block in my arms became denser, heavier as I tried recalling every detail of those glossy *Better Homes and Gardens* pages. *Now were the cinder blocks stacked in rows of three, or was it four?* The cinder block sank into my ribcage, displaced my lungs. *No, rows of two or three, maybe, but stacked how high?* The planting bed's simple-enough design twisted violently, became something gothic, javelin steeps and facades. *But if I go and do all that, will there be room for posts?* The sun beat savage drum solos on my skull.

"Boy, you hear me? Do it right. Do it right or so help me God!"

Right before my damn arms went slack, I heard a series of tight rubber bands snapping in my head—*PLIK! PLIK! PLIK!* I fumbled that cinder block and smashed up a finger between it and the planting bed. A cold wire of pain cut through me, lashed every tender nerve something awful. I bit my tongue down to the sinew and didn't cry. Crying could only confirm weakness.

Grandma rolled her eyes and said, "Oh lord."

I jerked my finger from between the cinder blocks. A blood blister swelled and strained against the crushed nail.

I told her, "I can do better."

"No you can't." She spat and folded calloused hands on her belly. She looked like a sack of lumpy yams in that oversized sundress. "I'll get men to do it. Spoiled backs fail. Strong backs don't."

I wasn't fool enough to say anything out loud, but who in the whole wide world would be desperate enough to work for an ogre like Grandma? I wondered who as my blood dried black on the cinder blocks.

NOBODY. NOBODY WOULD work themselves half-dead building Grandma's dream garden—nobody but those Morlocks. They ate cold, gelatinous soup straight from the can, chugged pints of cheap rum, chewed cigarette butts, pissed in pickle buckets, and sucked their black, mossy teeth while advising *Good pussy is best eaten like ripe honeydew, slurped clean, gnawed down to the rind and all that.* Grandma treated them like gentlemen—at least for a little while.

On that first day, I rode my bike over to the lot and found Morlocks farting around. Grandma was sitting in her lawn chair, primping a chocolate brown doo-wop wig, fingering a mother-of-pearl necklace that reflected sunlight in great bursts. She entertained an audience of a dozen or so. Morlocks sat on milk crates and moldering stumps. I could only wonder in what desolated corners of Hell Grandma had posted *help wanted* flyers.

"Boy!" Grandma called me, waving her flabby arms in a rare fit of good-natured excitement. "Hey, boy! C'mon, now!"

I leaned my bike against the horse apple tree and approached Grandma with slow, cautious paces. Quick movements might've ruffled her good mood, sent it soaring away.

Grandma whopped me square on the rump as if I were a goat fattened for slaughter and introduced me to the Morlocks. "Hey, y'all, this my grandson, Avery," she said. "He grows like them goddamn weeds—just as worrisome and ugly too."

Most of the Morlocks just grunted or coughed while others seized into painful smiles. One enthusiastic dude mashed his hands together—*CLAP! CLAP! CLAP!*

Me and the Morlocks went to work planting these pitiful lily bulbs Grandma had gotten cheap from Soulard Market. The bulbs were shriveled and coated in dust. Weak roots stretched from their tops and bottoms, tangled like thin pubic hair. This was a dreadful crop—no wonder Grandma had gotten it for a steal—but me and the Morlocks kicked shovel heads into hard earth, used them anyway.

Grandma didn't holler, or cuss, or say one mean word the whole time. She just sat there with her rough hands folded in her lap like a deacon's meek wife, the smile on her face brittle as the costume jewelry around her neck, all flimsy accessories.

If she was plotting something, I sure as hell couldn't tell what—but at least she was quiet. No science fiction leeches would suck at my flesh.

The Morlocks quit right at sun down, hunkered in the dust, and passed a Black & Mild between chapped lips, even though only four lonesome rows of lily bulbs had been planted in a good day's work. Black & Mild smoke was a blue specter, phasing through me, infiltrating my head and lungs slowly. Fireflies drifted through the smoke, scorched holes in the air like fever dreams.

Grandma stalked the crooked rows of lily bulbs as the bronze dusk darkened into leaden blue. I couldn't really make out her expression under those silky, synthetic bangs. But then a firefly grazed her cheek, bathed her face in an eerie glow and revealed her jagged scowl. That gruesome mug would've been perfect for an old school *Tales From The*

Crypt cover. The firefly crumbled into a speck of ash and floated away. My fight or flight switch *CLICK-CLICK-CLICKED*.

The Morlocks kept right on belching smoke, unaware of the acidic scorn primed to spew and blister their hides raw. Sweat on my back cooled into ice, scored my spine with chills. I couldn't tell if I was more fearful or excited. I wanted Grandma to eviscerate the Morlocks with sharp words, flail her tongue like a scythe, cut them down, heads tumbling under the horse apple tree. Somebody else had to get it besides me.

The Morlocks remained whole that night. Grandma just called out to them in a tired but nice enough voice. "Hey! C'mon in y'all! Let's get some hot grease on them guts!"

Inside the corner store, the Morlocks lined up and accepted paper plates heaped high with fried catfish, butter pickles, yellow onions, cold spaghetti, and slices of Wonder Bread as payment for their labor. Not a one of them complained about the catfish being freezer burned. None of them begged a red penny. The soup kitchens were closed. Nobody else would feed them or sponsor their half-assing. They happily sopped grease off their plates with bread crust, smacked skin right off their damn lips, licked fish bones bare and sparkling. A gangly Morlock jabbed a plastic fork at Grandma and said, "Miss Margret, you sho'll put the good foot in this one."

Grandma adjusted her wig, bared a grin full of alligator teeth, and said, "Oh, that ain't nothing. At least somebody will get a taste, 'sides the rats."

"Well, I sure hope y'all had plenty," Grandma said while ushering Morlocks out of the corner store. They grunted appreciation and poked toothpicks between what teeth they had. She slapped on this earnest-Girl-Scout smile and watched them shamble into the humid, suffocating dark. Once they were gone, she rapped my knuckles with a wooden stirring spoon and told me, "Boy, go'n get that garbage. Now."

BACK AT HOME, Grandma held Granddad's hand and told him about her ideas for business-saving renovations, whispering in his ear, urgently, as if talk of new toilets and formica counters were honey-coated epithets. Granddad was laid out in a hospital bed, nothing but limbs jutting at wrong angles underneath a shaggy quilt. The living room had become his infirmary, catheters in the magazine bin, saline pouches in the fish tank, dark stains crushed in the carpet. I kept a post at the door in case he needed to be rolled on his side, so he wouldn't choke on his own vomit. I never looked him in his face. If I did, he would sputter and tremble, newly afraid of me as I had always been afraid of him.

She told him, "I got men who will work themselves to the bare, bloody hoof for a steaming pot of coffee and a fried baloney sandwich, sho'll will." She thumped him on the shoulder lightly, "Now watch me, Henry, just watch me. I'll have them pans burning up, them fish jumping, that cash drawer fit to bust."

Granddad replied only with that grating cough, junk rattling in his chest, drill bits, bullet shells, razorblades.

"Watch me turn a drop of piss into good wine," she said. "Watch me—you'll see."

GRANDMA'S CORDIAL SPIRIT didn't last long. Me and the Morlocks dragged cinder blocks through the back lot like Egyptian slaves, built those romantic *Better Home and Gardens* planting beds in tight grids, and she told us *Y'all is the sorriest excuses for men I ever set eyes on. Can't tow a line. Can't bust a grape.*

Me and the Morlocks attacked spiked battalions of weeds, snapped rusty shears through thorned stalks as devil's eyelashes and milk thistle stung our ankles. She watched all this and told us *I could turn the dead fresh out they graves and see them hustle ass faster than any one of you lazy, good-for-nothing bastards.* At the end of each day, she never thanked us, never patted us on our sore and knotted backs. She just told us *I hope somebody loves you, be it Jesus or the motherfucking Easter Rabbit, cus' I sho'll don't.*

Grandma's insults stuck in my head like hot shrapnel while the Morlocks easily slipped her bombastic volleys of meanness with well-timed shrugs. Muttering *awww-yeah-yeah-yeah*, they paid her no mind and finished their jobs. It's like they knew Grandma was only confirming pathetic truths everyone else in their lives had already discovered about them. Besides, I don't think they could beat her cooking.

Grandma dogged the Morlocks out all day, every day, but fed them like courtesans at the fold out dinner table. They were happy enough working for a hot plate, as if the salmon croquettes were dredged with diamond dust, neck bones ruby studded, 24-karat cornbread. Every last man grinded hard for that plate—except for this one dude called Skyhook.

Skyhook was tall, long and lean as a bullwhip, and strong too, but he was plain lazy. He slow-bopped up to the back lot at about noon each day, still wearing fly gear from the grown folk's lounge, gator loafers and wide lapels. His breath stank of sour beer. His eyes were bloodshot like he had busted a few capillaries, a shameful sight in the too-bright day. I imagined if I took a circular saw to his skull, I'd find his brain floating belly up in a puddle of cheap vodka, bloated and tinged green like a pickled egg. Even staggering around the back lot half-drunk, Skyhook was sly enough to pass off his fair share of work.

He ran game on me and his fellow Morlocks daily. I hate to admit it, but I was the easy pickings. He used unspoken tenants of elderly respect as a bludgeon. *Hey, youngblood,* he'd say with twisted metal and smashed bottles at his feet, threatening to slash and gouge his shiny loafers, *go'n snatch up that broom and do your big brother a solid.* He'd grind palms in his lower back, grimace for my benefit. *Ooo-weee, that evil world done knotted my spine something terrible.* I'd nod like I totally understood, grab the broom, sweep.

When I was done, he'd always lock my hand in both of his, the fresh manicure on his nails taunting, and say something like *'Preciate you, youngblood—we sho'll need about a thousand more good Christian soldiers like yourself out here, not all these ne'er-do-wells and hoodlums.*

I was desperate enough to accept his encouragement, even if it was the by-product of crass manipulation.

Skyhook suckered other folks into handling his work by distracting them with bright bars of gossip mined from the grown folk's lounge.

He'd clutch a trowel in his fist, tight, and say stuff like *You know Jay and them? Yeah, buddy, I heard they was 'bout to hit a lick.* He'd scrape a rake across a few rocks and say *Oh, yeah, best watch yourself out here. I heard them dick-boys be lurking. Got old Bennie Williams caught up. Twenty-five years to life over some dope and a pea-shooter, on that third strike. Yeah, buddy, on that third strike. Now ain't that 'bout a bitch?* He'd pull a ripcord, get that leaf blower hacking and sputtering, pull a dude in close, and tell him *You heard about little miss Chloe? Yeah, nice girl. School girl. Educated and everything. Well, times is tough, homeboy, and she out here slanging that cat—I ain't lying. If you feeling blue, holler. She'll do it for a button, sho'll will.*

Skyhook, the sheisty bastard, did less than nothing and still got a place at the fold-out dinner table, up until that one afternoon where his loud fashion sense did him in.

THE SUN HAD a vendetta that day. Sunbeams were iron rods, thudding heavily, battering buildings and flesh all the same. Leaves roasted yellow and brown, fell off sagging branches, crunched under foot. Cups of water roiled, brewed, and transmuted into stale armpit sweat. Ice cubes popped, evaporated on contact with the atmosphere— they could not save you.

The Devil himself was stunned by the heat. He took off his wife-beater, plopped on the asphalt, and devoured a watery Sno-Cone, ivory horns thrusting skyward, tongue lolling. On a day like this, Grandma needed the compost heaps turned. She certainly wasn't taking no for an answer. Sho'll wasn't.

Those compost heaps were open-air digestive tracts, belching and gassing nefarious fumes. Stick a shovel in that muck, and the stench would claw your face to the wet, glistening bone. Even worse than that, those compost heaps blasted heat, had a bad habit of combusting into foul smoke and fire. The clumps of horse manure at the heart of each pile were good as grenades. None of that concerned Grandma. Fanning herself with a crumpled Chinese food flyer, she hollered, "Who's gonna turn them piles of shit?"

I sure couldn't. I was swinging a machete, trimming a yew bush, ratcheting my shoulder off, my skin bubbling like roofing tar.

She kept on hollering. "I know y'all hear me. I said who's gonna turn them piles of shit?"

Those Morlocks sure couldn't. The heat had whooped them long ago. They were catatonic in the dust like horned lizards, sweat sluicing over ridged brows.

"Hey! Who's gonna do it? Goddamnit—I said who's gonna turn that shit!" She spat. "Y'all can be lazy and trifling as you wannabe! Somebody is turning that shit!"

That's when Skyhook bebopped up to the back lot, G'd up in this cocaine-white suit, cool as a snow drift, everyone else sweltering. That fool even had a yellow umbrella slung over his shoulder to boot— daffodil yellow—glowing.

Grandma sneered at Skyhook and chuckled, low and mean. She pointed and said, "You—I got you now," she waggled her finger. "Oh, I got you, Sky-guy, Fly-man—whatever the fuck it is they call you." She pointed at a compost heap, heavy with fruit flies. "Go turn that shit."

Morlock eyes settled on Skyhook. I wiped resin off my machete. Skyhook brushed his sleeves, closed his umbrella, and produced a handkerchief from his breast pocket with a flourish. He thoughtfully wiped his forehead and neck, leaned on his umbrella as if it was a cane, and pointed to a bird's nest hanging from the general store's rain gutter. "I thought you wanted me to get that bird nest," he said. "You know I'm long and strong."

"If you're so damn strong, turning that shit won't be no problem," Grandma countered. She rocked herself out of the lawn chair. She shuffled over to the plastic container of random tools we had, fished out a pair of rubber gloves, and tossed them to Skyhook. "Here—you don't want that funk under your nails."

Skyhook caught the gloves and actually snapped them on. He propped his umbrella on the side of the general store and made for a shovel.

"Nope," Grandma said. "No shovel," she eased back in her lawn chair. "Got to turn it with your hands. Let's it breathe better."

Skyhook scrunched his eyes shut, as if he was working through a calculus problem, reckoning vectors of shame. He opened his eyes and saw the Morlocks smirking like school children, anxious to see a prank play out. He ripped off those rubber gloves, thrust out his chin, and told Grandma, "I ain't getting my hands in no shit. You ain't clowning me."

"Then you ain't eating," she said. "Don't think I never saw you running that big mouth."

"Oh, I'ma eat, alright." He faced me and the Morlocks. "Watch me come right back up in this bitch and get a plate."

"I wish you would," Grandma said, a growl in her throat. "I sho'll wish you would. I'd love to burn your ugly, mooching ass to the ground."

"See you at six on the dot, Miss Margaret, and you know I like my greens with a little extra pepper." Skyhook performed an elegant bow, retrieved his umbrella, and strutted off into the broiling day.

Grandma watched him go, chuckling low and mean. "I'll be damned," she said. "I'll be damned."

SKYHOOK ACTUALLY SHOWED up at six on the dot like he said, decked out in evening attire, a red velvet suit, and a for real pocket watch, silver chain and all that. The Morlocks put down their crispy snoot sandwiches and murmured. Grandma fixed her wig, folded up her lottery numbers, and cracked a blank smile before charging off to the back. I quietly finished my potato salad then positioned myself in the room's center, equidistant to the rear exit, front exit, and emergency axe.

"Good evening, my fine-feathered gentlemen," Skyhook addressed me and the Morlocks. The Morlocks replied with grumbling, but I didn't say nothing—speaking to dead men invites plagues upon the soul.

Skyhook fixed himself a plate, a double snoot sandwich, two heaping scoops of potato salad, greens with that extra dash of pepper. As he took a place at the head of the fold-out table, he fashioned his handkerchief into a bib and hummed a falsetto tune—Isley Brothers, I think. Smart Morlocks scooted away from him, chairs shrieking against linoleum.

Skyhook took a bite of his snoot sandwich and uttered his boldest, commercial-ready *Mmm! Mmm-mm!* He smacked his lips, licked his fingers one by one, and said, "Ain't nothing like a home-cooked meal, you hear me? Where's the chef so I can give her my regards?"

"Right here," Grandma said. She had a bottle of lighter fluid in one hand, matches in the other. "Right here, you great, greedy motherfucker." She charged at Skyhook and squirted up his chest and crotch with the accuracy of a gunslinger. Skyhook knocked over his plate and lunged at her, but she had already flicked a match across calluses on her palm. After that *WHOOSH!* Those orange flames licked air, and there was this stink of scorched rags, Skyhook's growling and cursing, the *WHAP! WHAP!* as he slapped himself stupid, trying to kill the flames.

You know he wanted to punch Grandma out, but he never got the chance. She put a boot in his ass and hustled him out the front door. He stumbled over the stoop and sprawled out on the concrete, smoldering.

She rattled the rusted iron front gate shut, lumps of muscle hard in her biceps. In husky breaths, she told Skyhook, "Hope you enjoyed. Tell all your folks. Y'all come back soon, you hear."

FUNNY THING WAS, Skyhook did come back. Me and the Morlocks were busting up dead stumps with hatchets, Grandma telling us, "Swear I'd get more use out of each and every one of you if I shredded you into mulch, raggedy bones and all."

When I saw Skyhook bebopping up the sidewalk, I gripped my hatchet tightly, ready to sink it in his skull. He was back for revenge—I knew it—twin pistols in his belt, thick sticks of dynamite lit behind his back. When Grandma saw him, she didn't flinch. Her lips curved with an awful, knowing grin. She relaxed in her lawn chair and hollered at Skyhook like they were old pals. "Hey, Skyguy! What you know, good?"

Skyhook strolled closer, put on the airs of a great philosopher, and said, "Man can't survive on gin and tonic alone."

Grandma jammed a fist in her chin and told him, "That's the wisest thing I've heard in years."

Silence dissolved their banter. I noticed Skyhook wasn't dressed so clean, so fly. He wore a plain baseball cap, a dingy t-shirt, and stone-washed jeans, worn in the knees. The only thing loud about him was his belt buckle, a chrome fist studded with rhinestones. Maybe Skyhook didn't want to risk anymore of his good clothes around Grandma, either that, or she burned the swagger right off him, as if it were a layer of ethanol, nothing of substance. Skyhook took off his hat and swatted a nagging mosquito. He said, "Miss Margaret, I was stopping by to see if you needed me."

Grandma gazed up at Skyhook with a naked look of wonder, as if he had sprouted a shining unicorn horn from his forehead. "Need you?"

"That's right."

"Need you." She shook her head thoughtfully. "Now what would I need with a high-saddity piece of fluff like yourself?"

"High-saddity?" Skyhook grimaced and flapped his hat at the accusation. "N'all, that ain't me."

"Yeah, you is. Dress it up, dress it down, you is a high-saddity piece of fluff." Grandma affirmed her instincts with a nod. "I got no need for a man who can't tell his dick from a stick in the dirt," she waved an arm over at me and the Morlocks, "got enough idiots as it is. All full up." Skyhook's jaw flopped open in protest, but she raised a hand. "I swear you could fish through pumpkin guts and find more brains." She chuckled low and mean. "Need you? Man, you've got some nerve." *THUNK!* A hatchet fell, severed a root. Skyhook scrunched his hat and turned away, and just then, Grandma said, "Come to think of it, I might need a scarecrow."

Skyhook wheeled around cautiously. "A scarecrow?"

"That's right. A scarecrow." Grandma got up and stood belly to belly with Skyhook, studying his eyes like she was going to kiss him. She reached up and squeezed his shoulder. "You tall enough," she prodded his ribs, "bony enough," she blew in his face while he suppressed a snarl, "ugly enough," she patted him on the chest. "Oh, yeah, you'd make a perfect scarecrow." She turned to me, "Yo! Avery! Go'n get a milk crate, two buckets, and some rocks. Big ones."

I dropped my hatchet and moved quickly to get all that stuff, Morlock eyes darting after me. I set the stuff at Grandma's feet. She wiped her mouth, kicked over the buckets and said, "I never said put the rocks in the bucket. Don't you ever listen?" She took her teeth out of my neck and deftly turned on Skyhook. "Now, stand on that crate."

Skyhook closed his eyes for a moment, revisited that worrisome calculus problem, and then stepped up on that crate.

Grandma said, "Alright, good. Next, I need you to spread your arms up high. I said high. N'all, spread 'em higher, like a chicken hawk." Grandma placed one chunky rock in each bucket, put the buckets in Skyhook's hands. "Hold 'em tight. Hold 'em high. Right. Just like that." She beamed a smile in Skyhook's face. "Don't you know I'm growing tomatoes and peppers? Can't have them nasty birds tearing 'em down."

While the Morlocks went back to work on the stumps, busting them up, wrapping them with chains, and hauling them out of the ground, I had to mind Skyhook. The day grew long, and Grandma commanded me to toss more and more rocks in the buckets swinging at the end of Skyhook's fists. Evil tremors broke through his face and body as the buckets grew heavier, but he held on strong, didn't fall off the crate, didn't drop so much as a pebble. That wasn't good enough. If Skyhook's arm wavered and dropped, I had to punch him in his shoulders, right in the bolts, Grandma telling me, "Harder. I said hit him harder."

AFTER SETTING SKYHOOK straight, Grandma got harsher with the Morlocks. It worked. If used mops were left outside to mildew and attract gnats in black halos, every last Morlock had to march around the neighborhood, Salvation Army boots clopping on broken pavement. If any dude was caught bullshitting while bricks needed to be sorted and organized, Grandma made him chew asphalt and flex knuckle push-ups. And if that old dude puked, well, he knew where the sawdust was. With a few weeks of no-tolerance discipline, that abandoned lot was polished into something charming. Grandma figured it was time for Granddad to see it.

She jerked him around in a wheelchair, pointing at new additions, all the hidden jewels. A bright steel arch for roses had been erected and threaded with robust, green vines. "See that, Henry?" Breaths of blue star sparkled sapphire, hyacinth crowns bowed. "And how about this?" Celosia waved leafy blades of fire and blood. "Now ain't that something else?" A clutch of tomatoes was coming in, golden, swelling fat. "See it, Henry? See? I told you so, didn't I? Sho'll did."

Granddad just moaned as his head pitched back and forth.

Sure, that lot looked good, but I knew it couldn't last. I could see the Morlocks second-guessing themselves over the tiniest details. They found less and less pleasure in their labor or the meals that followed. I knew how they felt. I knew how it was to stutter over the easy steps, how a rake could become a monstrous, skeletal wing, flapping, fighting your grip.

So as the Morlocks passed their Black & Mild one day, I tried to tell Skyhook sorry.

"Sorry for what, youngblood?" He said, inhaling and narrowing his eyes.

I tried to tell him. "For the—"

He rolled his shoulders, raised a hand, and hollered to the other Morlocks. "Hey, y'all! Youngblood say he sorry!" The Morlocks boomed laughter. Skyhook snatched my hand, turned it over, and slapped me once, twice on the wrist. "Boy, I'm grown. I don't hold hate in my heart. Cain't nobody hurt my feelings."

NOTHING UGLIER THAN
GOLD ON A CORPSE

HANDSOME CHARLIE WAS beaten dead ugly, mouth pulverized into a mess of cracked teeth and bleeding gums, lips split, curling like old watermelon rind, tongue oozing out over a busted jaw, eyes swollen shut, round and dark as bruised plums.

The savage dudes who whopped Handsome Charlie stole his looks, but didn't have time to jack his bling. He was shining hard, plated in gold and platinum. Diamonds studded his ears. Chains laced his neck, talismans of power. But none of that junk warded off this epic beat down.

I didn't know what to do for him—I mean, I didn't even know if he was alive. I had no 1up in my cargo shorts. Social Studies discussed the ethnographic makeup of Inuits and how the Roman Phalanx proved impenetrable, but it had never covered what to do in case of finding a dude slumped and dumped behind a run-down chemical factory. D swaggered right into action, telling me, "Avery, my nigga, get his kicks."

I spat a severe, "What?"

"You heard me, fam." D nodded at the flawless, red Jordans on Handsome Charlie's feet. Of course a vain fool would leave a well-dressed corpse. "I told you get his kicks, those Jordans, los zapatos, ándale."

To be real about it, I was kind of jealous. My Shoe Carnival sneakers stank of ultra-concentrated toe juice and were falling apart like bad papier-mâché, but stealing a half-dead man's shoes was just plan dirty. I told D, "N'all. I'm not—"

D shoulder checked me and growled, "Scary-ass nigga." I only hung out with D because he was always willing to trade the latest PlayStation videogames for paperbacks from my dead uncle's comic book collection. I never thought our arrangement volunteered me as an accomplice in petty crime.

D hunkered down over Handsome Charlie and yanked off those Jordans with a grunt. He didn't stop. D's hands worked cleanly, efficiently, like starved rats, snapping every bright morsel of shine off Handsome Charlie's body. D stuffed all that loot in his jeans and then cut me with a razor glare.

"You ain't snitching, is you?"

There were neighborhood legends of snitches being force-fed nails and smothered in liquid concrete. I answered, "Hell no."

D draped a platinum chain over his arm as if he were a salesman at a department store, and I was the fussy old lady looking to buy. The cartoon skull on his t-shirt leered at me. "If you ain't no snitch, take it."

"But I don't want it."

"See, I knew you was a pussy-ass nigga." D's smile was mean and playful. "Old ho-ass—"

I snatched the chain off his arm and said, "Shut up."

He folded his arms and said, "Now put it on."

"What?"

"Put that shit on, my dude. I ain't fucking with you."

The chain felt wrong in my fist; it would feel twice as wrong on my neck.

D started in again. "Oh, then you a punk-ass nigga, old—"

I wanted to head-butt D, crack his face like plaster, but I snapped that stupid chain on instead. Morals and nerve crumble quickly under the hammer of eighth-grade bullying. Fair enough, the chain felt too tight, throttled me like a choker.

D considered me with a sort of cautious pride, shook out his dreadlocks, and snapped a gold chain on his neck. He told me, "On the real, though, you cool people, Avery. So I'ma' let you live this time." He pulled his bike off the ground and swung a leg over the seat. "My oldhead dropped this shit on me: open mouths welcome open graves. Don't forget, my dude." D shot down the alleyway, tires rumbling on the cobblestone.

THAT CHAIN MIGHT as well have been barbwire, the way it bit into my throat, but I didn't take it off right away, fearing D would feel a disturbance in the ether, instantly know I had broken our contract. I turned my back on Handsome Charlie and swung a leg over my bike seat, but when I stamped on that pedal, the gear chain slipped. I fumbled the bike over and wrestled with it—that's when I heard Handsome Charlie trying to breathe. It sounded like the dry rattle at the bottom of an empty spray-paint can. For real. I should've turned and looked. One pitiful look might've kept his body and soul fused together.

But instead I closed my eyes and imagined a gang of crows falling upon Handsome Charlie like dark arrows. They'd rip at him with super-strong talons. He'd come apart easily at the joints like a life-sized action figure, limbs popping free. The crows would fly away and bury him on a mountain, a place with tough-ass stones and wild flowers. They'd ditch him somewhere. I wouldn't have to deal with it.

Handsome Charlie kept trying to breathe. I didn't want to turn around and ask what happened. I didn't want to see his eyes open in wet, snotty half-moons, like some helpless, newborn thing. I didn't want that intimacy. Shame lashed me as I hefted my bike and ran.

I COOLED OUT at the junk yard. Anxiety made the summer light harsh and gave scrap mythical aspects: ruined trucks were the exoskeletons of giant beetles, engine blocks all heads lopped off a hydra, dust-licked and rotting. A full-grown fox jagged across the oil-slicked asphalt, mange flickering like muted flame, yellow teeth jutting from muzzle, primitive blades.

A rodent's fear of predators and open spaces walloped me in the chest. I crawled through a section of industrial pipe and hid in the Grungy Van. The Grungy Van was a Vortex of Gross, reeking like mildew and buttsweat. One time I found a King Cobra bottle full of dark piss sitting on the dashboard. Another time, the console was stuffed with bloody gauze, shed like lizard skin. No need to talk about those used condoms artfully glued to the ceiling, dangling, flaking ectoplasm. This time, I found tinfoil origami glittering on the passenger seat, a crane, a frog, a few star-shaped flowers.

Handsome Charlie might as well have been dying on a faraway continent, but dread rumbled through my chest, thudding hard, rattling nerve and bone. I unfolded the tinfoil origami, refolded it into compact squares, ripped them into tinsel. That elemental dread diminished, became a ghost-story dread, unpleasant but surreal and kind of exciting. I could've pretended Handsome Charlie was an awful vision brought on by heat exhaustion and too much black cherry Vess if it wasn't for that stupid chain burning radioactive around my neck.

My reflection glowered at me from the review mirror, dull and blurry, the chain a bright scythe edge separating head from shoulders—and I really don't know why, call me an idiot, but goddamn it—for one hot minute I really thought I looked like somebody, a caliph mean-mugging for hieroglyphs. I'd have royal guardians at my back, a high priest hexing my enemies, pretty women serving me cheese sticks from an ivory bowl.

A grimy hand shot through the driver side window, tore at my sleeve, and jerked me out of that daydream. Franklin, the junk yard owner hollered, "Boy, I done told you too many times 'bout bullshitting on my property!"

Before inheriting that junkyard, Franklin got his jaw busted in an amateur heavyweight boxing match against Grady "Sledge Hammer" Jones. The bones never healed right, leaving Franklin with the grimace of a Rock' em Sock 'em Robot shoved into early retirement. The crooked planes of Franklin's jaw grinded as he said, "I ain't playing with you!"

I kung fu parried his hand, combat rolled over the seats, drop-kicked the passenger side door, and hopped on my bike. Franklin hollered, "Hey! You little shit!"

He didn't normally get so pissed when he found me loitering. Either threads in his battered hippocampus were unbraiding, unleashing sooty veins of rage, or he totally knew. Totally knew I was a lying, thieving coward, flossing a dead man's shit.

AS I BIKED down Grand, that elemental dread resurfaced and mutated into guilt, infecting heart and head with paranoia. I expected pharaonic curses to fall out of the sky and split my skull like a ceremonial sword. But necrosis didn't eat my flesh. That stupid chain didn't transmute into a snake and flash venom dripping fangs—n'all. Nothing bad happened at all. Life bullied by.

Fluffy shaving cream clouds replicated endless screen saver patterns. Oil-drum smokers belched rich, sacrificial fat. Morning glory vines strangled fences and barbed wire. Little girls traded secrets for Garbage Pail Kids cards and snorted big rhinoceros laughter. Prehistoric fruit flies sprinted from neck to neck, sucking up sweat and perfume, all that summer nectar. Out in front of a gas station, Miss Annette offered me a candy apple, delicate and pretty as blown glass.

I ate it in four giant chomps, planning to run before Miss Annette started rambling. Sugar lined my teeth, lush as fur, syrup melting on my lips. Miss Annette swatted at a fly then nodded at a couple of teenage girls sitting on the stoop of a ruined storefront across the street, cut-off shorts riding their hips, thighs plump, sizzling in the heat.

Squinting fiercely, Miss Annette shook her head in a mix of open jealousy and admiration. She said, "Oooooo child, these girls be so damned thick, like they don't drink nothing but buttermilk." Wringing her hands, she gave a sorry smile. "Sho'll put a bony nag like me to shame, don't they."

I shrugged and wiped my mouth.

Miss Annette swiped a few sticks, speared a few apples, rapid-fire. She pointed a stick at me and pursed her lips. "Get a good one, now, you hear me? Trust and believe, a fast girl will get you killed. Don't let no short-shorts be the story of your life."

I nodded studiously and biked on.

I spotted D on the corner by the liquor store where dudes bragged and hitting a lick became legend. D held up the clutch of jewelry he stole from Handsome Charlie as if it was the head of a rival warlord. Neighborhood dudes crowded D, slapped him on the back in celebration. D had those Jordans on and his shirt off, skinny chest straining with false pride. He talked all kinds of shit to his crew, "Pay the cost or get tossed, that's what I tell a pussy-ass motherfucker."

D saw me, and his eyes sparked. "Yo!" he hollered at me. "Yo, my nigga, Big A!" The neighborhood dudes cast their attention on me, expecting me to corroborate D's fictions.

If I was a different kid, I would have taken off my shirt and joined D, braying *No lie, me and that cold-blooded nigga Big D, we whopped that bitch-made nigga—Wham! Wham! Wow!—brains on the motherfucking pavement.* But that wasn't me. I turned and biked through traffic, D's shouting like stones pelting my dusty hide. If a monster truck had hit me, splattered me under sixty-six-inch tires, I wouldn't have been sorry. Not at all.

LATER THAT NIGHT a collage of bad dreams thumped through my brain. Me and D were on the corner in front of the neighborhood dudes. Big D held up a string of diamonds stretched in a lattice between his hands. Those diamonds fused with Big D's voice, winking rhythmically as he spoke, fiery rainbows breaking inside glacial walls. I couldn't hear what he said. It was all radio distortion, static grinding.

In the next dream, Miss Annette was dragging a trash bag full of gristle and bone behind her. She shook her head and said *live and die like these damn flies,* her mouth and voice out of sync, something inside the trash bag writhing.

Next, there were men with bricks for heads, their expressions all angry crayon scribbles. In the last dream, Big D nudged me in the ribs and said *Speak on it, my nigga. Tell these niggas what we be about, how we do. Go'n, tell 'em. Tell 'em what's up. Go'n.* I tried to tell them how hard me and Big D were, but when I opened my mouth, nothing but bent nails, razors, and black scabs fell out, no brags, only a cloud of rust.

Truthfully, Little D was just a punk-ass scrub who ripped off some helpless dude, and I was too much of a pussy do right. I woke up with tacks in my belly, a sense of urgency sumo-squatting on my chest, that stupid chain tighter than ever.

OF COURSE, HANDSOME Charlie was gone when I returned to where I had found him. But it was eerie, like he had never even been there, not a chalk outline, not a sock, no cop on the case—just up and gone.

I wondered if he was somewhere crumpled inside a drum of corrosive acid, flesh made jelly, bones disintegrating into Alka-Seltzer fizz. Maybe his ghost was stalking me, observing my weaknesses, plotting to cut an incision in my back and steal my soul. Maybe God's hand came down, wearily batted away a few clouds, pinched him up. I couldn't call it.

I stared at that patch of tall weeds where Handsome Charlie had lain and concentrated as if it was a Magic Eye portrait, like the weeds might shift and reveal a message, give me a definite answer. The garbage and dead hornets and mean-looking spines remained constant, random, plain meaningless.

Maybe he had gotten up, walked away, and soon, he'd catch me in the street, a gnarly club in his fist, that stupid chain attracting him like a beacon—THAT STUPID CHAIN. I didn't want it in the first place. All it did was brand me a coward. I tried to snatch it off, but the clasp stuck. So I tore at it, threw it in the dust.

When I got home, I found the smallest laceration on the side of my neck, weeping blood. I cleaned it, slapped on a band aid, but it still hardened, became a scar. And it's not like anybody looks at me funny—to this day no one knows it's there. Only me. That scar is tiny, nothing more than a tooth mark from a beast that bit but couldn't kill.

CAULDRON

BIRDS, CATS, RATS, and dogs had sense enough to fly, burrow, and lope out of the storm's path. But the folks lined up at Teeth's backdoor were senseless and unashamed. Hard rain soaked through their socks and drawers, mud sucked at their sneakers and boots, wind ripped at their coats and hats, blasted umbrellas crooked. Those fools didn't budge or cry for help. There were about fifteen of them, Buddhas in obsidian and bronze, calm and sturdy, heedless of tornado sirens and elements, as if orderliness could stave off a feral sky, keep gusts of wind from flinging them over defunct factories and condemned houses.

I watched from the kitchen window as those folks conducted efficient business, hands snapping from drenched sleeves quick as snakebites. This grossly tall dude named Greenbean guarded the door while my video-gaming-buddy D served product. Rain slanted and pummeled D right in his sullen face. He shook the cold and wet out of his dreadlocks and growled all species of *Fuck* and *Motherfucker!*

Once transactions were complete, survival instincts returned. Those folks hustled away with goods in hand only to be absorbed by the dust and furor like wisps of steam and—

WHO THE HELL WERE THEY?

Busted umbrellas, scarves, hats, and hoodies cloaked faces— but I knew these folks. I did. I pictured them as mystery figurines packaged in black plastic. Tearing open a wrapper might reveal the desperate old dude who sold melted candy bars outside the liquor store, or that sweet, overbearing lady who once gave me a packet of antibiotic ointment for razor bumps on the back of my neck. These folks running grim errands through the center of a storm could only be my neighbors and nobody else. I was already writing eulogies on the ledger of my heart.

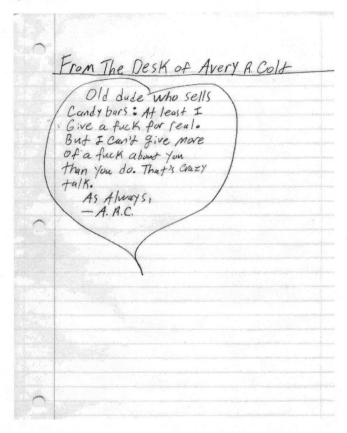

I was a punk-ass fifteen year old who didn't understand this form of mass suicide at all. Teeth didn't suffer the same dread and confusion. He cooked a batch of crack on the stove, stroking the chemical broth with a fork, forearms ripping, blue flames hissing and clawing that cast-iron skillet. Harsh vapors polluted the air, filled my lungs with razors. He caught me moping by the window and said, "Don't make no sense, do it?

"Unh-hunh, I know, but let me put it to you like this: fiends make the best waiters, maids, and soldiers." He moved the skillet to a cold grate, lit a cigarette with flame from the burner then clicked off the range top. "They'll take shit all day long, don't understand the word no, and would shoot they mama for a solid dollar. I'm dead serious. Throw a pebble on the ground, I swear these motherfuckers would suck the meat off your big toe."

He took two luxurious drags and peeked through the curtains. His grin revealed a pair of sleek gold fangs.

"Ain't no surprise they out here in this bullshit, finna ride that tornado like whoa." He nodded. "Mm-hmm. Crack will eat holes in your brain, lil' brother. Real talk. Hit that shit, and you might fuck around and put your dick through a brick wall, you be so damned hyped—but you already knew that."

Teeth was dead wrong. I didn't know anything, even though gossip about crack was so common it could fit into a form letter.

Gossip A: Did you hear? Mister or Miss_____ is on that shit.
Gossip B: N'all! The Hell you say! That ain't (him/her)!
Gossip A: Mmm-hmmm. Sho'll is, honey. (He/She) been fucked up since—
> *a) tragic loss of employment*
> *b) tragic loss of loved one*
> *c) tragic loss of etc.*

Gossip B: I knew they was doing bad, but not like that. Well, I surely will—
> *a) pray for them*
> *b) look out for them*
> *c) duck that mooching motherfucker like the living plague.*

I heard about crack all the time. It was everywhere, in our bread, in our basements, on our backs, in our sinuses, in our blood, a community health concern, the cocaine flu, yet I had never actually seen the stuff until that day.

I had just wanted to trade D *Final Fantasy 7* for *Tekken 3*, and then the storm hit, and Teeth said there was work to do, and he told me *Hold up, boy. You don't know me, but I know you. Let me holler at you for a minute.* So I was caught up in the bullshit too.

TEETH TOOK ANOTHER drag off his cigarette, tapped ashes into a beer can, and told me, "So like I said, I know you don't know me, but I know you. You ain't even gotta tell me your name." He laid a firm hand on my head as if he was a faith healer. I wasn't about to fight him, find he kept a shank in his belt, a snub-nosed pistol in his sock.

He proclaimed, "I was gone for years traveling the world, not for drink and women and all that nonsense—n'all. I traveled all over the world for—uh, what they call it—enlightenment. Mm-hm. Enlightenment. I conversated with wise men from throughout history, sho'll did. I chopped it up with Mr. King and Malcom X and the Dhali Lama and Ghandi and Moses, Nebuchadnezzar, even Jesus himself—eyes of fire, wild afro, skin like coal." Thunder crashed. Teeth tightened his grip. His fingers stank of sweat, nicotine, and bad pennies.

"Them wise men saw my true purpose, laid secrets at my feet, gifted me with powers. Believe me when I say powers. Sight beyond seeing, the sixth, seventh, and eighth sense—all that." I was thinking *bullshit* when the kitchen lights flickered out. Lightning flared copper in the window. Ions sizzled through stale air. I tasted ozone. Mean thunder beat like war drums *BA-BOOM! BA-BA-BOOM!* Teeth spoke my name. "Avery—Avery Colt."

A cold blade carved figure eights in my spine, but I pretended to be unimpressed by his theatrical timing. The lights clicked back on. I brushed his hand away and told him, "Yeah."

"Goddamnme, I knew it! I knew it!" Teeth howled. His enthusiasm would have been charming if it wasn't for those fangs. "After I came back from my travels, I seen you bullshitting with my nephew, and thought to myself," he tapped his chin, "don't that little yellow bastard look mighty familiar?

"Matter of fact, me and your folks go way, way back. Sho'll do. I used to buy Wonder Bread from your grandmama's store every Monday, and your Granddady—you know one day I was feeling ornery and stole two cans of beans, and that crazy nigga pulled a machete on me—now what kind of shit is that? Damned if I know, but that ugly, rock-headed motherfucker sho'll was bad. How a girl pretty as your mama ever came out his seed, I'll never know.

"When we was young and hip, she used to kick it with a brotha'. Sho'll kicked it. That girl would come on through, drink up the last drop of wine then dip when we passed the hat, like she never even touched the stuff, on some sheisty shit. I swear. After your uncle passed, it was all bad. She turned boosie den' a mug, had her nose up in the air. But I ain't mad at her. Sho'll ain't."

Teeth leveled a blunt glare and asked me, "Now, your mama ever tell you about your uncle?"

No. Not at all. Mom avoided talking about my dead uncle as if his memory could signal demons, would have hooves clopping on our roof, claws tapping on our screen door. A different kid would've been more curious, more demanding. A different kid might've felt cheated, but not me—how much could I feel for a man I'd never know? We shared blood and a name, but nothing else. So I only had one good detail for Teeth. I told him, "I don't know—Mom said he worked in pharmaceuticals."

"She said what? Pharmaceuticals? Boy, she always been mighty clever, your mama, but that's a goddamn shame. Pharmaceuticals? How she gonna give you that man's name but not the truth? See, if you ask me, secrets keep you sick."

BUT I COULDN'T see it—Mom kicking it with a dude who rocked gold fangs and moved crack. Once when I was a little kid, I cliqued up with a shady cabal of local badasses and got caught throwing rocks at cars cruising down Grand. After using one of her slender, fashionable belts to emboss my butt and thighs with zebra-print patterns, Mom gave me a short, bitter speech. A short, bitter speech that she had prepared for a man I'd never be. She told me *Avery, I won't suffer for what you choose to do. If you let foolishness tear a bite out your ass, you're good as dead. That poison is slow and quiet.*

I gave you life. Your death is your own.

*

TEETH FUSSILY RATTLED that skillet of crack like it was fresh Jiffy-Pop, lit another cigarette, then glared at me for a long, hard minute, his rude appraisal radioactive, crisping my skin. "Now, boy, I have plenty to tell you, but I can't go handing Boo-Boo the Fool Keys to the Kingdom." He sat on a stool, crossed his legs, turned his cigarette up, and postured like an intellectual. "Let me ask you this: you ain't one of them folks who takes a rag and washes they feet and ass before washing they face, is you?"

Sometimes. But I told him, "No."

"Good. Question number two: If a ball rolls in the street, do you chase after it?"

"Hell no."

"Smart man. So let me ask you one more thing." Teeth got up, yanked my wrist, and dragged me over to the stove. He tilted that cold skillet towards me. The crack inside was dingy yellow. It looked like fragments from a busted skull, shards of bone and powdery marrow. "Tell me, what do you see here?"

My mouth was dry, dead moths under the tongue. I told him the truth. "I don't know."

He pointed at me and said, "You sir, are correct. I'd give you a prize, but I'm fresh outta zoo-zoos and wham-whams." He casually scraped a nail along the skillet's burnt rim, collected cocaine residue, suckled his finger without a hint of shame. "Mm-hmm," he smacked his lips, "don't nobody know what this shit is. Sho'll don't, but use what the Good Lord gave you." He rapped the side of my head. "You'll see.

"Some folks might see death and poison. Other folks see the Devil's intentions made flesh. Mm-hmm. But understand, folks like you and me—we have imagination—that's the big difference.

"If you hollered at me, saying *Yo! Teeth! What you got in that skillet, man?* I wouldn't be shy. I'd tell you I set that pan on fire, get that shit boiling, and I got me some brand new suits, some thick women, a down payment on a house, more jewels than you could count all bubbling out that pan—Bloop! Bloop! Bloop!"

Even under the influence of a contact high, I couldn't see pearls popping from the skillet like hot grease. I couldn't see prosperity. I could only see a woman's hand rising from the chemical broth, skin blue as ice, thin wrist laced in fat rubies, fingernails severe as razors.

Teeth smiled and opened his hands in an oratorical pose. "But now I'm about to blow your mind. What's setting in that pan is more than diamonds. I'm talking dynasties. See, your uncle, my partner, he knew something about them wise men and much more. He knew about blood. He knew about heritage. He knew about legacy. You hear me? He—"

Teeth was building to a larger point, but shouts and screams cut him short. He muttered, scowled, and turned to the window. Barbs bunched in my gut.

I TURNED TO the window and watched as D fought a girl with blue hair. She boxed competently, jabbed, set up hooks to the body, pivoted and pushed, slipped wild punches. She stuck him once, twice, clean busted his nose. Snot and blood bubbled in his nostrils. The rain washed his face, preserved two cents' worth of his dignity. He swung. She slipped, stuck him once, twice, stepped out of his range, sucked in two breaths, adjusted the chunky rings on her knuckles.

Folks hollered, "Whoop his ass!" They pumped umbrellas like spears and demanded more. Greenbean blocked those folks from jumping in, his height and width good as a brick wall. She ducked a haymaker, tried to pivot, but the mud sucked off her sneaker. She stumbled to one knee, dropped her hands, and D rushed, suddenly athletic and sure footed. He clutched her head, knee'd her in the face, once, twice. She scrambled through the muck on all fours as he sneered and kicked her ribs.

Teeth clucked and said, "We ain't playing with you today, partner. No sir. We ain't playing."

THE ONLY GIRL I knew with blue hair was Erika Banks, my sister's used-to-be-best friend. At seven Erika and my sister thrashed razor scooters across playgrounds, ran over the feet of old men, crushed toes, and giggled. At ten they challenged curfew and spun orange glow-in-the-dark hula-hoops around skinny hips, starlight on braids. At twelve they coco-buttered their legs, rubbed and buffed thighs so shiny you could see your reflection, rode in cars with grown-ass men. At fifteen they lifted King Cobra from liquor stores, smoked weed in abandoned buildings, and one time, stumbled home so jacked up and high they nearly burned down the house with a hot comb. At seventeen they fought over a busted-ass dude, pulled razors on each other while he watched. Now Erika and my sister had identical scars across their bony chests like matching tattoos. I had heard Erika had been tripping off That Shit since her nephew got shot. But I didn't want to believe it.

D CONTINUED TO kick Erika's guts in even after she had crumpled on the ground. I wanted lightning to fall like a blade and cut him in half—but what kind of coward was I? I stood there and watched D beat her without intention of stepping in and getting beaten, stabbed, or shot myself. I closed my eyes and performed crude surgery, snapped open my breastbone, pitched my heart and every organ responsible for sympathy into a fire. I traded decency for survival like everybody else. Once D was satisfied, he let Erika get up and collect herself. She staggered off into the dark mist, that blue hair spiteful of humiliation, whipping and blazing in furious winds. At a safe distance, she turned and cried *YOU PUNK-BITCH!* I didn't know if that insult was meant for D or me.

GREENBEAN SHOUTED AND snapped. The crowd in Teeth's backyard bagged up their bloodlust and reorganized the line. There were fewer of them now, but how could the remaining folks be such golems, so single-minded? Craving and desperation had scooped out their brains and filled the cavity with canned peaches.

D tromped through the muck, kicked open the door, and hollered, "Fuck!"

Teeth turned to D with the worn patience of an unheeded tutor and said, "Now, D, tell me why you didn't pull your gun? You could have avoided all that wrestling if you had put that thang in her face from the jump, told her shut the fuck up, whoomp, whoomp, wow, she gets her shit, you get her money, and nan' one of y'all look like motherfucking fools."

D bowed his head and massaged his scalp. "That bitch got sick all over my kicks." There was vomit and muck on the cuffs of his jeans and sneakers. He took off his sneakers and lined them neatly by the wall. He lamented, "They was Jordans too. Limited editions, can't get 'em in stores."

Teeth jumped to his feet and snatched a small pot off the stove. "Boy, you mean to tell me, you got a gang of money just waiting at your back door, and you worried 'bout some damn shoes?"

D peeled off his wet socks and snarled. "You can't get them shits in stores, you hear me?"

"N'all," Teeth said. "I ain't heard shit." He raised that pot overhead as if it was a cudgel. He wasn't threatening so much as he was ridiculous, brooding like an overworked grandmother scorned by dirty carpet and a sink full of dishes. "Go'n before I finish what that bitch started and bust your head wide open."

D had already been clowned once that day. He had no need for any greater indignation, so he wiped a drip of blood from his nose, put on his sneakers, and resigned himself to the chores of a basement-level crack dealer.

"Boy, don't never forget who feeds you. I will put you out. Have you on the streets, bald-headed, wearing a trash bag, eating fried baloney sandwiches."

D shook his dreadlocks and grunted, but he didn't say another word. Resentful yet obedient, he opened the door. A violent wind barged inside, lashed whips against our backs. I watched D trudge back into the mud and—fuck n'all—I didn't feel sorry for him. He didn't need to be out there anyway. Not him, not my neighbors. Nobody I loved.

TRUTH IS I was curious about my dead uncle, but mostly I was more terrified he—THE OTHER AVERY—would get all salty one day and leave the netherworld, wanting his name and life back. I feared waking in the night to the stench of rotting meat and finding him ransacking my bedroom, his putrefying fingers spreading grease over my comic books, gooey maggots trickling from his suit sleeve, fouling my PlayStation, corrupting save files. Hunks of meat would fall off his bones as if he had been slow-roasted in Hell. He'd come close, slap me affectionately on the cheek with an ice-block hand, and rasp, *My turn.* Fuck all that. Teeth could offer me whatever, but I wanted no part of a legacy born from suffering.

I NEEDED TO get the fuck out of that crack house. I needed to bury myself in a bunker before that storm ripped all fools in two, but Teeth blocked the door—he wasn't done hollering at me. Sho'll wasn't.

He pointed out the window behind him and retched, "See that? This is what the fuck I'm talking about, lil' brother. Stupid-ass niggas don't know how to wipe they own ass, but they wanna call the shots. Any nigga can act hard and drop a hammer, but it takes a keen mind to survive in this game." He spiked a finger in his temple three times.

"To tell you the truth—an old dummy like me had to learn that the hard way. Oh yeah. Your uncle would tell me, *T', don't be spending all your money on clothes and jewelry—that's how you get caught up.* So what I do? Spend all my money on clothes and jewelry. I wanted to be shive, goddamnme. Then he'd shake his head and be like *T', don't be partying, messing with those girls and pillow talking.* And guess what I did? That's right. I'd get paid and get my shit wet. Fuck what he had to say about it."

Teeth casually lit another cigarette, inhaled, and squinted as smoke curled around his weary eyes—but damn, didn't he hear that mean thunder? *BA-BOOM! BA-BA-BOOM!*

I lunged for the door, but he stepped in front of me and thumped a fist into my chest. "Hold up, lil' brother. Hold up. We ain't done yet. Nothing out there to see no way. Like I was saying, boy, a nigga like me only wanted a smooth ride, fly clothes, and some hot pussy, know what I mean? I had all the taste of a simple nigga, and simple is as simple does. But your uncle, he was on some other shit. He'd be like, *T', stack that bread. Save your money. Invest in a business. Don't play yourself, partner. You make wealth, not money.* Right," Teeth tapped my chest, "but I never understood him, stayed on that dumb shit. But you—you his blood. I owe this to you.

"You don't know me, Avery, but I know you and your family very well. Peep game, lil' brother." Teeth jaunted over to the refrigerator, swiped a baggie of crack out of the freezer, and tossed That Shit to me.

When I caught That Shit, my whole arm went numb and fell right off.

Teeth was unfazed and went on. "The flip is easy. I front you, you break 'em off. We'll start you off small. Run that twenty, I'll give you five. That's fair enough and easier than selling a Mr. Goodbar."

I reattached my arm, tossed the baggie back to him, told him, "No."

He thumped that baggie on the stove and then gently pointed a question at me, "Now, Avery. If you see a dollar on the ground, would you pick it up?"

"What does that have to do with anything?"

"All I'm saying is you sho'll would pick up that dollar, spend it too, so why don't you hold something. I'm telling you it's easy."

"No."

"You won't even try? That's all I'm asking. Try."

"I said no."

"Now that's alright. We're not all made for the street hustle. What I really need is somebody square to keep a little dope in they house. As you can see, this current set up ain't—what they call it—sustainable."

I restated my point. "I said fuck n'all."

He stepped back, stunned. "Oh, it's like that?"

"Hell yeah. It's like that." I opened the door and walked out on his punk ass. Rain slapped. Cold sliced. Teeth stood in the doorway and shouted curses after me, called me all kinds of bitches and motherfuckers and pussies. He could do what he wanted. I owed him nothing.

Those folks concealed in scarves, hats, and hoodies laughed and pointed. Greenbean lurched towards me—but what did I have to fear from him when the storm would kill us all? D was ankle deep in mud and too defeated to say shit.

I turned to curse Teeth right back, but then a battering-ram wind whopped me in the gut, lifted me off the ground, slammed me into a fence. I blacked out for a good minute. Those monstrous drums rumbled and roused me—*BA-BA-BOOM! BA-BA-BOOM!*

The line of folks had been scattered all over, their scarves, hats, and hoodies ripped from their faces, revealing who they were. Beneath a smoldering tree split by lightning there was Tay Clark who ran a daycare out of her home and Old Bobby who'd fix your car for fifty dollars flat. By an overturned car there was Get It Steve who had stolen and pawned my bike no less than five times. There was sickly Mr. Terrance who won a workman's comp settlement from a chemical company. And then there was Miss Denise, a knockout choir soloist and flea market queen, being hurled down the alleyway like tumbleweed, big bones, plump ass, and all. They were all there, and so many other folks I knew, beaten senseless.

I should've snatched Tay and Old Bobby from under that tree, pulled Get It Steve and Mr. Terrance to their feet. I should have leapt, reached out and anchored Miss Denise, kept her from getting smashed against the cobblestone, swallowed by the furor. I should have helped, but it took everything I had just to run and save myself.

TEETH'S STORY

FRAILTY AND FLAB didn't keep neighborhood elders from demanding respect. They upheld social order on sagging shoulders and corrected trifling, ungrateful slobs with threats of old-school punishment. Grizzly, retired men threatened to rap knuckles and slash switches across backs. Mean, goat-bearded women promised to slap lying tongues into the stratosphere. I was afraid of walking past their porches with nappy hair and wrinkled jeans. Their anvil-headed judgment squashed ignorant-ass punks like me.

Neighborhood elders claimed to practice tough love, but they held a special, unforgiving contempt for dope dealers. They had seen crack ravage generations. Hot pipes split lips, chemical clouds suffocated kin, rocks avalanched, crushed sons and daughters.

When a dope dealer got shot, nobody sang praises at his funeral. When he got out of prison, nobody baked him peach cobbler, welcomed him home. When his mind turned on itself, nobody counseled him. They watched as paranoia and guilt turned feral, grew wing and talon, savaged skull and breast. When a dope dealer's family withered, neighborhood elders grunted and said *That's what them lousy motherfuckers get.*

So you have to understand my dread when I found a pickle jar full of crack hidden in my dead uncle's closet. I feared his death wasn't enough to clear the karmic debt he had charged to our bloodline. I imagined elders chewing iron nails, banging hammers, erecting crosses of shame to crucify me and my folks.

Mom never talked about her brother, as if the mention of him would beg hellfire to fry our sorry asses. If I asked her anything about him, she'd stomp and cuss me bald. If I told her I had touched That Shit, she'd chop off my hand, boil it, feed fingers to pigeons. Nobody would discuss Grown Folks Business with me except for Teeth.

Old dude was a defunct dope dealer and prison mystic who rocked gold fangs. He claimed that my uncle had burned out whole blocks beside him back in the day. After coming home from a long prison stint, Teeth tried to revive his drug game. But that shit didn't work. He came out dusty and broke. Young thundercats feared that his failure would infect them, rot the gold around their necks, raise lesions on their limited-edition sneakers. They shamed him. Neighborhood elders mocked him, told him *White Castles is always hiring. They love shitbirds. They sho'll do.* So Teeth switched up his grind and earned bread by selling junk and tall tales to chumps. For real.

He'd post up at Fairground Park, raise a busted pair of clippers, holler *I know this don't look like much, but this thing right here sheared Samson's hair, made him bald as a baby's backside, weak as a kitten, ripe for the butcher—you hear me?* He sold bus passes that never expired, sardine tins that multiplied overnight, boom boxes that blasted God's voice.

Most folks laughed at him or cussed him out—but the folks who spent money—they listened for a hot minute and walked away with a dazzled look in their eyes, as if they had stumbled out of a crypt and couldn't adjust to that new light.

Baby Keith from around the corner got conned into buying a pair of cheetah print sunglasses for twenty dollars. The fool said those sunglasses let him see bad news before it hit. A grizzly, retired man snatched the sunglasses off his face, crushed them in a fist, and said *A blind man can see trouble coming, if he know where to look.*

Now I didn't believe Teeth's bullshit, but after hiding that pickle jar full of crack in a crawl space, and having stress dreams where neighborhood elders circled me, stripped me naked, and clobbered me with red bricks, I slanged that shit in my backpack and searched for him that very next day, hoping I could snatch raw, bloody answers from his fangs.

I COULDN'T FIND Teeth fast enough. That pickle jar full of crack felt like a boulder in my backpack. Anxiety squeezed air out of my lungs as I entertained grim visions of neighborhood elders leaping off their porches to serve me reckoning. I thought Mr. Simons, the master landscaper and botanist, would drop his garden shears and grind my bones under his riding mower; I thought Miss Jacqueline, the caterer and historic food scholar, would drop-kick me into a bubbling vat of hot canola oil.

I biked to Fairground Park without trouble, but I didn't find Teeth by that track where middle-aged women powerwalked and curled jugs of water. I didn't find him near the cement rink where roller skate kings and queens busted disco moves and cut neat curlicues. I didn't find him by the abandoned pool where a race riot once broke out.

Mean, goat-bearded old women told stories of square-headed white boys brandishing crow bars and baseball bats, cracking heads, cracking backs. Once it was over, those women carried their sons, cousins, and brothers back home, rubbed frozen peas on swollen faces, soothed bruises with cool hands and soft voices.

I found Teeth smoking a cigarette by the lake, near the medieval-looking stone bridge. He sat on a worn leather trunk and bobbed his head to the static rasp of a beat-up little radio set between his feet. He snapped out of his mellow vibe and burned through me with a glare.

I propped my bike up against a tree, shifted my backpack, approached him. He studied my frown, cut off his radio, tapped ashes in his palm. He told me, "Boy, you been waiting on me? Yes you was. You been waiting on me your whole life. Don't hide your face now. Don't holler. Don't run."

TEETH LAID HIS game on me before I could even ask him about my uncle or that pickle jar full of dope. He told me, "Young man, burdens trouble your heart—that's plain for everybody to see, but I'll get your mind right. Sho'll will. All I ask is that you listen—can you do that much? Just listen, and I'll make those burdens lighter than a feather. You'll fly high, once we through. You'll see. You'll fly high—but don't block out my light. "

He licked his thumb, pinched the cherry off his cigarette, tucked the butt behind his ear. That hard shine on his gold fangs made me think of him in a past life, raiding pyramids and shucking bracelets off bleached bone.

"Now when you jammed up for ten, fifteen years, there ain't much to do but lift weights and read. You sho'll can get your hands dirty if you want to, but even a chump like me know better. I seen them cats swindling and killing each other like they ain't had enough nonsense out in the streets.

"So I'd lay up on my cot and watch them cats bust heads and slash throats over soda pops and candy bars, and I say to myself *N'all. I don't want no part of that. I'm too damn old. Too damn beat. N'all. Lemme me just go'n head here and read this damn book.* And that's all I did. Read and read and read.

"I set down and read the Bible 'bout a hundred times—sho'll did—and more than that, I read stories from all over the world, picked the brains of poets and prophets from China, India, Africa, and they all had one thing in common to say: you don't ever come back home empty handed. I took that to heart and trained my eye to spot treasures men forget. Now I'ma' show you one not everybody gets to see."

Teeth hopped up and snapped open the brass buckles on his trunk. He rummaged through the junk. I was expecting a hot deal on Cleopatra's comb or a panther's eye—I expected him to pull out anything except an ornamental hunting knife. Red fur covered the bone-handle. Bright sunlight banked off the blade's tip.

"Bad, ain't it? You might think you need a nasty son of a bitch like this. Keep them wild niggas up off you—but that ain't my point. You go running 'round swinging this motherfucker at just anybody, and it'll end up in your own damn back, sooner or later." He ran his nail along the knife's edge. It sang an eerie note.

"Oh yeah—I ain't lying. This motherfucker is guaranteed to take a thousand lives once it taste blood—and you know what the bitch is? The last death will be yours. Now shut up and lemme tell you something about it."

TEETH'S EPIC SAGA

I.

BUT FIRST, I gotta tell you 'bout these folks who mastered all creation. They had the game licked. Bees brought honey to the lips of our people. Animals bowed beneath blades. The sky wept at songs, soaked the earth in that good, good rain. Yams and wild flowers came popping clean out the dirt. Common rocks yielded gold and jewels. Men stood tall, brawny backed and strong in the trunk. The women were so damn beautiful, you'd turn to pudding trying to look them in the eye—boy, I ain't lying! They was honey-dipped and thick.

Now whenever you on top, there always go'n be somebody's hating-ass waiting 'round the corner to knock you down. So don't act surprised when I say a tribe of giants became jealous of how the Masters of Creation were blessed. They waged war, stripped power from our people, and left them in the cold and dark. You can master creation, but that don't mean you can't get that ass whooped.

Quicker than I can snap my fingers, life became hard. Bees coveted honey and stung lips. Animals grew wild, broke blades under claw and hoof. The sky ignored the songs of our people. The earth dried up and cracked. Homes buckled and collapsed. Men lost faith and became weak. Women withered under all that sorrow. Charms broke. Our good people suffered God's wrath.

You best believe that cold took a tighter hold, settled damp in lungs and bones. Brothers killed brothers. Men whored they wives.

Women shamed they children—and more than that. The ancestors jumped up out they graves, wandered that wasteland, and questioned each and every descendant.

What the Hell is wrong with y'all? How in the Hell y'all let this mess happen? After everything we been through. After everything we done did for y'all. Shit. After everything we done. Goddamn, goddamn, goddamn. . . .

II.

SO THE ELDERS put they hands together and prayed for heroes. Folks say a star flashed bright in the sky that same night—and soon after—five virgins found themselves with child. Three days later, each woman gave birth to a healthy baby boy. They fed them boys milk and stew—and in just one night they all grew into full-grown men, big and strong, long wooly hair, hot coals in they eyes, all that. You already know they was blessed with sacred powers.

Zabari had a hide of iron. He could bust boulders with his fist and wrestle tigers to a stalemate. Tuma could hurl his club over the horizon and call yams out the ground with a slow, sweet song. Cayman could bust through three shields with his spear, whistle, and change the course of rivers. Khari could stitch wounds with the life lines from his palm and hit an ant's eye with his arrow. Akachi could snatch humming birds out the sky with his net and turn gristle into good meat. Goat, chicken, jack rabbit—whatever you want.

So them elders gathered them youngbloods and told them about a mighty, gold bull that lived in the Badlands. If those boys could hunt the gold bull and take his meat, hide, and bones, they could bring a new age of plenty. Zabari, Tuma, Cayman, Khari, and Akachi thumped chests and accepted that challenge. They was cocky as could be—you hear me? Dead cocky.

But the wisest elder warned them boys and said *We know you bad as they come, but we ain't never seen you struggle a day in your life. Not a goddamn day in your life. What do y'all think you can do for us without knowing pain and the seduction of death?*

I die when they shear my hair. I die when they cut me with a look. I die when they call me out my name. I die when the groceries is high. I die when the lights cut out. I die when they spit on my brother, turn a cold shoulder to my plight. If you love me like you say you do, you'll suffer. Child, you'll suffer with me and not say a damn word.

III.

ZABARI, TUMA, CAYMAN, Khari, and Akachi tracked that gold bull to the Badlands—and I ain't got to say it. You already know bad news was coming 'round the corner. Now that bull was no ordinary beast. He was ornery, strong, and cunning as I don't know what. He juked and jived, led those boys to death, one by one.

That gold bull led Akachi into a cave full of sharp rocks and spiders. That boy got lost and never saw the light of day again. That gold bull led Khari into brambles, growing thicker and meaner with every step, ripping flesh clean off that boy's bones 'til he was nothing but string and gristle. That gold bull outmatched Cayman, blunted that boy's spear tip with his invulnerable hide. When that boy went to the river to drink and summon his strength, a great lizard bit him, dragged him down into that deep, dark water. That bull made Tuma eat mud 'til he couldn't breathe no more. Now finally, that gold bull went toe-to-toe with Zabari—but he couldn't best that boy—Hell n'all!

Zabari grappled the bull, took him by his horns, lifted him high in the air, and body slammed him—*BAM!* Knocked the piss out that motherfucker! Dropped him so hard the earth shook. That gold bull lay defeated, but like I said, he was no ordinary beast. So before Zabari could break his neck and avenge his brothers, that bull spoke, talked all that shit.

That bull snorted and told him *Boy, you may eat of my flesh, drink of my blood and gain incredible willpower. You may use my bones to build homes that cannot be demolished by nature or man. You may use my hide and craft charms that protect you from vengeful gods. You may take the fire from my heart and light the dark. You may break my ribs, fashion a knife, and reign as king.*

You might do all that, but some day, after you think the battle's won, and there's no enemy in sight, folks will come to fear your power. Power will change you—don't think it won't. You will turn your knife on your brothers. They will call you arrogant and ruthless. The men you rely on will stab you in the back, take power for themselves. They will beat their drums with your bones, drink broth from your skull, pull scriptures from your tongue, burn them. They will do evil until they too are struck down. Knowing all that, you still want to break my damn neck?

TO BE CONTINUED.....

TEETH TOLD ME, "That's all I know. I can't say if the boy was successful or not, but I do know that this same story gets told in a lot of different ways. In some stories it's not a gold bull that them boys chase, but it's a fox, a bird, or a shooting star—though that ain't the point." He laid the Dagger of One Thousand Deaths on his thigh, relit his cigarette, and took a long drag. "N'all, that ain't the point."

I folded my arms and told him, "That's the dumbest thing I have ever heard. You can't end on a cliffhanger like that, and plus, what do you mean you don't know what he did? How else would you have that dagger if he didn't kill the bull?"

"What do you want me to tell you?"

"Zabari or whoever put up with a lot bullshit for a little bit of power he couldn't use."

"But at least he had choices."

"Right, and they both sucked."

"You ever heard the saying 'act like a motherfucking fool, and I'ma' treat you like a motherfucking fool'?"

"Sounds familiar."

"See, boy, that's your problem. You think you smart, but you don't know shit." Teeth finished his cigarette, picked up the dagger off his thigh, and pointed it at me. "Now is you go'n buy this knife or not?"

"Man, please. Do I look like I have money?"

Teeth laughed. "N'all—boy you look raggedy as fuck, like you just fell off the back of a pumpkin truck, with your country, baloney eating-ass—but that ain't my problem." He picked his fingernails with the dagger and glared at me. "You can't be wasting my time. I ain't got shit else. You need to buck up, beg, borrow, steal, and pay tribute. Knowledge ain't free. Niggas died for this shit."

Teeth kept pushing me, and so I gave him the only thing of value I had. I unzipped my backpack and tossed him that pickle jar full of crack. He caught it. His eyes bugged out as if I had thrown a troll's head in his lap. He held it up to the light. The rocks shone dingy white and jagged, like the splintered teeth of rodents.

Teeth asked me, "What the fuck you want me to do with this?"

I shrugged and told him, "You know better than me."

Teeth searched his pockets for another cigarette, but he couldn't find one. He lowered his head, looked up at me with a furrowed brow, and said, "Boy, let me tell you something. You know I was walking down the street the other day, and Miss Annette—you know Miss Anette—the sweet thing who be selling candy apples and sno-cones? She seen me the other day, and you know what she did? She spat dead in my motherfucking face. Dead in my face. Snot and everything.

"Her cousin smoked up his job, his house, his car—and guess who she blames? Like I can break anybody's back by my lonesome. The bitch is everybody loves you when you handing out loans, paying tuition, feeding folks. But then you fall flat on your ass, where they at? You just a oldhead then. You just the scum of the motherfucking earth. Now tell me—am I right or wrong?"

I shrugged. "I really don't know."

Hurt broke Teeth's face as he jabbed a finger at me. "Now you been standing here for 'bout an hour, staring me dead in my face, nodding your head on some *UNH-HUNH, UNH-HUNH* shit, and you ain't heard a goddamn word I said, lil' brother. Not a goddamn word. I said I'm through. I already told you—I'm through."

He stood, thrust the pickle jar of crack in my face, and said, "This shit right here, it ain't nothing. It ain't what folks think it is. But this shit—it ain't nothing at all." He chucked That Shit high and far. We both watched as it turned in the air and hit the lake's surface with an explosive, depth-charge splash.

Teeth turned to me, put his hand on my shoulder, leaned his weight on me and said, "Lil' brother, don't play games with me. Listen when I say this—I'm through."

CUT OPEN THE VEIN

GRANDAD WOULD WINK and fill an empty refrigerator with milk, eggs, meat, and cheese, call plump catfish from muddy banks and hustle them into a hot fryer, fertilize tomato plants with his dandruff, turn solid coin out of crushed beer cans, squeeze water from stone, resurrect busted engines with a thump and growl, honor old covenants of earth, blood, and motor oil. He could sew a loose stitch into a suit and clothe a naked man, roll breadcrumbs into a loaf and fill empty stomachs. But only a fool would mistake his kindness for weakness.

He could and would beat the breaks off a motherfucker—I'd seen him do it enough, beat a man with fists, feet, baseball bat, revolver butt, or frying pan, crack skulls against counter tops, choke a man until air hissed out from ears and eyes, his body sagging like a sack of beans.

He told me once: *Have one damn thing worth a shit in this world, and there'll be a bastard waiting round the corner, pipe in his hand, wanting to take it from you. Folks will rob you and clown on you too. Make a damn celebration out of it.*

Granddad could do all that. His bones could not.

GRANDDAD'S ABILITIES WERE expansive and strange, but I had a sound theory: his powers came from past lives. I read the birthmarks and scars on his body and saw the timeline. He had been a hunter, a slave, an architect; a hammer, a mason, a dragonfly; an alligator, a gladiator, a furnace, belly full of coals, head of smoke and rioting flame—this was true. He was not a man, but many. At the age of sixteen, I was a dumb-ass kid equipped with no arsenal of hard-earned survival skills, no past lives.

I was Avery R. Colt of the Joy Stick, Master of the Shoryuken, Reader of Comic Books, Lord of the Dirty Bathtub Ring, Disciple of the Wobbly Horse Stance, Burner of Toast, Conqueror of Succubi and Night Realms, Defiler of Sheets. I told you—I was a dumb-ass kid and comparing me to Granddad would've been unfair and cutting. But after the wake, my folks couldn't help themselves.

I MEAN, MY folks couldn't figure out what the fuck was wrong with me. I was supposed to evolve into a man like Granddad, but I hadn't grown much beyond the larval form, had failed at erecting a chrysalis of iron and nails. Was my failure to mature caused by a lack of raw nutrients in the environment? A lack of magnesium and copper, boron and zinc? Or was it contamination from the paint chips Mom ate while I slept inside her womb? Or were there congenital defects of character inherited from my absentee father, good as holes in heart and lungs?

My folks had an intense, scientific debate about it in the living room. Grandma offered the first hypothesis and blamed video games. "It's the radiation," she said. "It's shrinking his stuff—that's why he's so ornery. If he keeps it up, his manhood will look like two raisins on a withered vine. Sho'll will." She concluded her findings with a firm nod.

My older sister Yell disagreed and said, "N'all, that ain't it—it's them white people at school. They got his head twisted in knots."

Colette Thompson, Mom's best friend since eighth grade, waved a dismissive hand and said, "No—we have to at least respect his mind. I don't believe he's so simple." Colette had just lost fifty pounds on a cabbage soup diet. A sharp slit up the side of her black dress revealed one bodacious, muscular thigh. "The issue is easy: it's too much salt, fat, and sugar. All that trash makes you thick in the middle and thick in the head. Some boiled eggs and fresh kale would do him a world of good." Colette beamed a talk-show-host smile, smoothed her dress, flexed that juicy thigh.

Grandma, who had made platters of pig's feet, rib tips, chicken wings, and crispy snoots for the wake, pinned Colette with the evil eye and told her, "Now, don't you say another word of that hogwash." Grandma bucked in her seat. "I'm telling you once—not one more motherfucking word."

Colette looked down and quietly adjusted her pumps.

I spied on them from the dining room, and to be honest, they all looked strangely beautiful in their dark meditations, black veils falling over faces like soft shadow, smooth, shiny hair swooped up and cylindrical like the headdresses of Egyptian queens, this scene ready to be preserved in lithograph. But I still wished for ashes to fill their mouths and shut them the hell up.

"What he really needs is some pussy," Yell asserted.

Colette gasped, smacked Yell's arm, and shouted, "Young lady!"

Yell shrugged and said, "What? I'm for real. Beating off five hours a day will make any man blind, crippled, and crazy." She leveled a mean smile at Colette. "And don't come butting in—unless you gonna give him some."

Mom said, "Unh-unh," then finally gave her opinion. "What he needs is a good punch in the nose. If it was the last thing he did, I wished Daddy could've whooped him good. A soft ass makes a hard head feel—but what can I do with a half-grown man?" She shook her head and glared at her hands, disappointed in her own weakness. She used to discipline me, but once I got too tall, all she could do was stare up at me and shake her damn head.

Colette raised a hand with a pained look on her face. "I understand your feelings, but Avery's still a boy—must we be so backwards?"

Grandma, Yell, and Mom looked at each other then mean-mugged Colette and shouted, "Awwwww, shut the hell up!" Colette crossed her legs and thrust her chin in the air defensively.

Silence bristled for a hot minute, and then Yell said, "Avery couldn't handle him no way. Grandaddy was a roughneck. He'd sneeze and knock the boy down."

Grandma raised a fist and said, "My husband was strong. He'd holler and black that boy's eye."

Mom nodded and said, "That's right. He'd snap a man's spine with one look."

Granddad defended his family and corner store with ferocity. So many louts, thugs, and minor-league villains realized violent changes of heart by his hand. Excitement sharpened blades in each woman's cheekbones as they told stories about how he dealt Good Country Ass-Whoopings.

Mom said, "I was there when he smashed that whole jar of hot pickles over Chuckie's head. Chuckie had it coming, that dirty, conniving, left-handed bastard. Unh-hunh. To this very day Chuckie will turn tail and holler mercy if you wag so much as a gherkin at him."

Then Grandma added, "Oh, that ain't nothing. I seen my old man whoop a whole baseball team with they own bats. This other time, he made a man eat his hat, back, brim, and all—ain't that wild?"

Then Yell asked, "Didn't Granddady put his bare foot up somebody's ass?"

Suddenly animated, Colette pointed at Yell and hooted, "I heard about that one!" She kicked the air. "Wham! Right in the stinkpot!"

Grandma confirmed, "He sho'll did and caught a fungus too."

Mom, Yell, Grandma, and Colette all looked at each other and then busted out laughing. Hysterical tears dripped down their cheeks. I had a good story about Granddad whooping ass, but I didn't want to interrupt.

NOW HERE'S MY best story about Granddad handing out a Good Country Ass Whooping. A few years ago at the general store, Grandma was roasting lamb shanks, I was practicing knife skills on a carrot, and Granddad was smoking snoots when this geeked-up old dude stomped into the general store and talked shit. Dude was so high, I couldn't discern insults from gibberish, but Granddad found a few phrases worth a brawl.

Granddad talked shit right back, and when that didn't squash it, Granddad vaulted over the service counter, yanked old dude's collar, and cracked him with a nasty hook—WHOP!— dude's whole face exploded. I mean EXPLODED.

Eyes bulged, nose busted, teeth broken, tears, blood, and snot gushing all with that one blow. Granddad didn't need to hit him again. Dude would've fallen if Granddad wasn't holding him up by the collar. Dudes jacked up teeth had cut up Granddad's knuckles; Granddad considered his fist and old dude's ruined mouth. I dropped my knife. Grandma closed the oven door, put a fist in her hip, and said *Well, don't quit now*. So Granddad didn't. When his right fist was tired, he used his left. Dude sputtered something like *please*, but Granddad didn't stop. I don't think he could've if he wanted.

Once the beating was done and old dude tossed into the street, Grandma closed the store and set to fixing Granddad's hands. Granddad's knuckles were shredded down to fat and gristle. I gathered the peroxide, lighter, and clean rags. She gathered the sewing needle and spool of fishing line.

Grandma soaked a rag in peroxide, cleaned the grit and dirt out of his wounds. She sparked the lighter, dipped the sewing needle in flame, blew it cool. She thread fishing line through the eye, pinched the skin together around the deepest gash. Granddad tipped back a bottle of whiskey. Grandma patted his back and said *Get you another*. He did. She said *Have one more*. He did. She pushed the needle through his skin. The fishing line and Granddad's mouth jerked taut. Her stitching was deft and easy as if she was only patching a pair of ripped jeans. Granddad frowned and shook his head. Grandma said *I don't know why you had to do him like that*. Granddad said *I don't know why either*. Grandma said *Oh, don't fuss now. You got it. Sho'll do.*

BEFORE SHE LEFT, Colette stood on the front porch and asked me, Mom, Yell, and Grandma to recite the Lord's Prayer. Mom bit her lip. Yell sighed. Grandma rolled her eyes and said, "I don't have time for that nonsense."

Colette stood firm, opened her arms, and said, "C'mon, y'all."

My folks reluctantly formed a circle. I joined hands with Colette. Her grip was cool and dry. She led the prayer. I tried to follow, but I couldn't concentrate. *Our father, who art in Heaven*. Boughs of honeysuckles burst across a window ledge. The blossoms huffed perfumed breaths. *Hallowed be thy name.* Cicadas droned drowsy cantos. Sunrays cut. Wires of dread tightened in my chest. *Thy kingdom come. Thy will be done.* A butterfly landed on my knuckle. Creamy wings fluttered. Its touch agitated my skin. *On Earth as it is in Heaven. Give us this day our daily bread.* I let go of Colette's grip and turned over my hand. Another butterfly landed on my wrist. *And forgive us our trespasses, as we forgive those who trespass against us.* I closed my eyes. I couldn't remember Granddad's face. All I could see was his shredded knuckles and blood on the linoleum. My eyes burned. The butterflies crawled, agitated my skin. *And lead us not into temptation, but deliver us from*—I crushed a butterfly in my palm.

Yell caught me and called me out. "Boy, what are you doing?"

The bug's guts stained the cuff of my dress shirt.

Mom saw the mess in my hand and said, "It wasn't doing nothing to you."

Grandma chuckled and said, "It's just a bug."

So I crushed the other one.

Colette slapped my arm and asked, "What is wrong with you?"

Colette tried to slap me again, but I snatched her hand, twisted her finger. She howled and asked again, "What the hell is wrong with you?"

I let her go. It's not like I had a good answer.

PART III

NECK BONES

I HID OUT in the basement, thumbed through Grandma's recipe book, and waited for the fight to end. Mom's voice sawed through the basement ceiling. *Danielle, what is this?* Yell mumbled something. Mom jabbed back *Unh-unh. If it's in my house, it is my business.* I could picture bad temper ruining their straightened hair, strands curling in feral spangles, hard sweat on their foreheads, polished nails cracking inside smooth fists, lipstick embellished snarls. Mom hollered *Nobody is playing with you, little girl.*

Shame on me, but I wished they'd just kill each other and be done with it. Shouting thumped against the walls, belligerent and frantic as a trapped animal. I refocused on the recipe book. Bizarre cartoons complemented Grandma's recipes. Dapper, cigar-smoking razor-backed boars in tuxes strutted margins. Roosters worked cast-iron skillets next to the secret ingredients for dirty fried chicken, wings flapping, cockscombs slicked. A fat-lipped trout luxuriated in a pot of roiling stock and celery. Keep that recipe book close, and you could learn everything about bouillabaisse, whipped mashed potatoes with beef gravy, liver and onions, headcheese, all that classic, down-home goodness.

Grandma's precise and pretty handwriting even detailed how to debone rabbits and French racks of lamb. Her handwriting was the only thing boldly feminine about Grandma, how it curved and swooped deceptively. With hands calloused and hard as a gravedigger's, she swung mallets, wielded skewers and knives, hocked *motherfuckers* and *whores* at anyone who stepped inside her corner store and failed to buy a hot plate and show proper respect. Upstairs Mom and Yell volleyed *FUCKYOU*s back and forth. In my head I heard Grandma's specter hollering A*WWWW SHUT THE HELL UP!*

Grandma could diffuse their fights with a few mean words and a good meal. She would tell Mom something like *Go shove your fat head in the icebox. You might learn some sense.* She'd hit Yell with *You bad, but you ain't grown—keep on, and I'll cut you down to a stump, sho'll will.* Then she'd lure them into the kitchen and throw leftovers on the stove, greens and ham hocks, cornbread, pork chops panfried in bacon grease, neck bones.

Every time Mom or Yell parted their lips to hurl another blame, Grandma would spoon broth in their mouths, put forks in their fists, and tell them to go on and eat before all that good food got cold.

I figured Grandma spiked her food with mood elevators because after a small plate or two Mom and Yell's bickering became secondary to slow chewing, lip-smacking, and—eventually—cautious laughter. I wished I had Grandma's moments of matter-of-fact grace, but I had no such easy charm.

A door slammed upstairs. Mom wailed, "Avvvveer-ree! Avery! You better come get this little girl!" Once Mom and Yell's fights got physical, it was more pro-wrestling than anything serious, grandstanding, figure-four leg locks, loud, echoing slaps to the chest. If I let one kill the other, drown her in a sink, contuse her with a hot comb, it'd be completely my fault.

In those days, I was nothing but a trifling sixteen-year-old dork who wore the same musty Teenage Mutant Ninja Turtle boxer shorts for days in a row and pissed in tea jugs when the bathroom felt too distant. I had no business mediating the affairs of grown women.

I trudged upstairs and found them in the hallway, bullying each other in rough kickboxing clenches, hands on throats, nails in hair. At least no blouses had ripped; no skirts had flipped up to reveal intimate and unsettling seams of satin and lace. One time, I accidently grabbed a boob trying to break them up. My hand felt contaminated for days. I scrubbed and scrubbed my palm raw, but it still felt soiled.

"I'm right here!" I shouted and forced myself between them, jamming the points of my elbows into their chests. Hands whipped overhead like hawks, tore out chunks of hair and scalp. Scabs and regrets would harden by morning. Mom was the first to relent. She stepped back, put her hands on her knees, spoke slowly.

"Avery, you need to get this know-nothing bitch out of my house." She straightened up, gulped a breath.

Sincere worry broke across her face. "I'll kill her. Swear I will."

I nodded, turned to Yell like a tough guy, deepened my voice, and told her, "Yell. You need to leave."

Yell folded her arms and said, "No."

So I pleaded, "Please just leave."

She razed me with a hateful glare. "And who the fuck are you?"

"Yell—"

"—Avery, I said no. And if you touch me—"

I snatched her shoulders and pushed hard. She was bird-boned yet surprisingly heavy, as if her resentments had condensed, become rocks in her belly. She cussed me the whole way out the door—*you pussy, you punk, you bitch*—the gravel in her breath scraping my face. On the porch she pouted and asked me, very seriously, "When are you gonna get off the titty?"

Yell had it in her head that I was the favorite, but that just wasn't true. Mom considered me a lazy fool, and I considered her a bully—we just never got to swinging about it. Foul words fumed in my chest like noxious gas, but I couldn't call Yell anything nasty. Didn't want to spit diesel on the flame. "Forget you," was the best I had.

She told me to gobble a fat dick and skulked off down the block to shake fifth graders for lunch money and hitch rides with bad dudes—whatever it is grimy girls do.

Mom was inside using an antique hand mirror to try and get a good look at the fresh, raw bald spots on the back of her head. She cut me a worried glance and asked, "It doesn't look bad, now does it?" Her bald spots were red and shameful, but I told her what she wanted to hear.

IT WAS JUST Mom and me later that night, eating freezer-burned TV dinners in separate rooms. That processed mush was no better than charbroiled socks smothered in onion gravy. Mom couldn't cook. I suspected she never liked to anyway. Even when Dad was around she oversalted meat, overlooked tiny bones. She always burned the butter.

That TV dinner was unsatisfying, left me wanting real food. I looked inside the refrigerator, found nothing promising, lunchmeat slimy like the skin of some sightless, cave-dwelling creature, squishy red potatoes shaped like grubby feet, toes and all.

Saltines and tomato soup, bricks of ramen lined the cupboards. I settled on a stale Hostess cupcake hidden behind the microwave. I ate half of it and flipped through Grandma's recipe book.

I wanted mounds of salmon croquettes and dirty fried corn, hunks of fork-tender pot roast with crisp rinds. I stopped at Grandma's recipe for goat stew, struck by the cartoon, a witless lamb, roller skates on his hooves, careening into an incinerator's mouth, flame and smoke spewing. I only had that stew once, and truth be told, the goat brought for the slaughter wasn't that carefree.

TETHERED TO A post out back of the corner store, the goat was shaking, bleating, and shitting all over the asphalt. Grandma and Granddad were debating on the best means of quickly and efficiently killing it

Grandma flipped a wickedly sharp knife and said, "You slit his throat. Nothing fancy. Nothing to it."

Granddad loaded his revolver, spun the cylinder—*TAT-TAT-TAT*—slapped it closed, and then tapped the barrel on that goat's head. "N'all. You blow his brains out—what's quicker than that?"

"And ruin the meat? You crazy as Hell, just want to make a mess. See here," she picked up a loose, red brick, "might as well clap him with this."

This was nothing but fun to Grandma and Granddad. They were transplants from the country, scrabbling through the city. If they wanted greens, they'd grow them. If they wanted goat, they'd kill it—simple as that.

Granddad pointed his revolver at the goat and asked me, "Boy, what do you think?"

I was nine, and my underdeveloped brain couldn't decode this complex multiple choice question:

HOW DO YOU SLAUGHTER A GOAT?
A. Knife   B. Gun   C. Brick

"Well, boy," Grandma said, "which is it?" Her teeth and the paring knife flashed in tandem. I crushed moths and water bugs beneath my sneakers, but I hadn't worked up to this level of necessary violence, hadn't killed anything with skin and a heartbeat. I put my hands up and shook my head.

Granddad twirled his revolver and said, "C'mon, boy, let me lay him on out real smooth. In fact, I'll let you pull the trigger—how you like the sound of that?"

I didn't like the sound of that at all. My bladder was suddenly hard and heavy.

Grandma objected to Granddad's fast play and hollered, "N'all!" She flipped her knife up in the air, caught it, and pointed at me, "If you want to see it done right, you'll choose this knife. Ain't two ways about it."

"You'll choose this gun, if you know what's what," Granddad said.

"This boy don't know his ass from a hole in the ground," Grandma said.

They sniped at each other like that for a few minutes. Then Grandma grabbed the brick and raised it overhead. The goat bleated and trotted in a slow, frantic circle, succeeding only in wrapping himself around the pole, no escaping this back lot butcher shop. The reaper had come for him in a faded sundress and slippers. "Let me get him done."

Grandma brought the brick down. Hit the goat once, twice—*WHOP! WHOP!*—clapped him easy. His skull cracked and syrupy blood oozed from the wound.

Grandma smiled with carnal satisfaction. "There," she said. "Nothing to it. Can't make a meal without a little blood on the floor." Granddad took Grandma's knife, got a length of rope and field dressed the goat right there. He slit the goat from the rooter to the tooter, hung him from the limbs of a strong apple tree. Blood pooled on the asphalt.

Stunned silent, I placed both hands over my crotch and hung my head. Grandma smacked my shoulder and told me, "Watch. You better learn."

Granddad tore out the goat's guts, easy. He pitched the heart, liver, and kidneys into the alley. Cats gathered and ate, lapped viscera off the cobblestones. Granddad said, "Might as well let them have their fill. They don't get this often."

Seeing the goat shiver and bleed had soured my appetite but didn't bother my folks any. After the goat was butchered, processed, and stewed, Mom and Yell came over for dinner. They sat down at the table, draped paper napkins over their laps, dug right in. Not one nasty word was spoken over that meal.

After Grandma and Granddad died, we no longer enjoyed that kind of peace.

OF COURSE MOM and Yell wouldn't reconcile over stale cupcakes and gross TV dinners. I couldn't kill a goat, but I could cook a meal, sauté and roast soup bones, make a new covenant at the dinner table.

Determining the exact duration of petty grudges between Mom and Yell was a mystical art. I referenced star charts and lunar revolutions and concluded Yell would come back home in three days, enough time for me to gather equipment and ingredients, devise a tantalizing meal that'd make Satan spitshine his horns and take supper with the Holy Ghost. I skimmed the recipe book and settled on St. Louis's Best Pork Tenderloin for the main course. Only an idiot with two left hands could fuck that up.

First I needed good cooking instruments. Our everyday utensils were ruined, fork tines snapped, serving spoons battered, butter knives that couldn't cut butter. I imagined the quality silverware and single set of china we never used were hidden under Mom's bed, guarded by rat traps. So I went downstairs and searched boxes inside Grandma and Granddad's old room, careful not to disturb the gloom.

Boxes and boxes of junk crowded that space, as if summoned by a revenant pain that preferred to hide, fester, and grow in potency. A fat, green spider dangled overhead while I rummaged through rusted wrenches and screws, empty tobacco tins, glossy doo-wop wigs that reeked of Grandma's sweat—goddamn—smelled just like her, that bitter tang of constant toil.

Before long I found graters and tongs and scoops and sharp, sharp knives. Blades glowed softly in the midday light. I'd written a report on Japanese culture for school once, and holding those utensils, Grandma's most trusted tools, I was reminded of Tsukumogami— household objects that attain life after a hundred years and become tricksters who waste sentience on nasty pranks or worse.

I couldn't tell if my hands were trembling or if it was the knives themselves, plotting to slip and slice my fingers. I got the hell out of there before that revenant pain could spend any more time touching my thoughts, making me weird.

Clattering down the hall, I was afraid Mom would find me out, but she was too busy tossing Yell's room, scrutinizing Polaroid pictures with a sleuth's roving eye, popping heart-shaped locks off those old middle-school diaries, pitching thongs and short-shorts in a trash bag as HOWs and WHYs conspired in her head and offered this flat, confounding equation:

$$\frac{\text{Shaming}^{nth}}{\text{new clothes} + \text{private school}} + \frac{(\text{ballet}) \times (\text{piano lessons})^2}{\text{ass-whoopings}^{10}} \neq \text{perfect daughter}$$

She muttered and calculated, but none of it added up to her. I moved on quickly, not wanting to see the calculus she had on me.

Next I shopped for ingredients at the small, Arab-owned grocery store. The place smelled gamey and metallic. I shuffled through aisles of canned meat and passed a circle of Morlocks guzzling Kool-Aid Bursts and smacking bruised lips. Inside the butcher's display case liver and Braunschweiger sweated clear goop, honeycomb tripe flared translucent ridges. Chicken gizzards gleamed dark ruby.

The butcher thumped a mallet on the counter and asked me, "What you like?"

I was feeling ambitious, so I ordered the pork tenderloin, the gizzards, and one gauzy sheath of tripe. He wrapped up the meat and asked me, "You cook?"

"Trying to," I told him.

He nodded gravely then pointed at a bright red bucket of chitlins sitting in crushed ice. "You cook this?"

Grandma, Mom, and Yell used to cook chitlins for Thanksgivings. All I could think of was their quiet teamwork, Grandma scrubbing the stuff against a washboard, Yell rinsing it in cold water, Mom wearing plastic gloves and a surgical mask, holding the pale strands of flesh up to the light and pinching off any mysterious, dark flecks with a pair of tweezers, that barnyard funk when it got to boiling and rolling, looking like swamp snakes dueling in the broth. Believe it or not, it wasn't so bad served with hot sauce, mustard, fresh onion, and potato salad—melted in your mouth.

So I told him, "Sure, I can handle them."

I eyed up a pyramid of canned greens on my way out, but figured I would do better scrounging through what was left of Grandma's garden. After hiding my goods in the basement deep freezer back at home, I grabbed a pair of shears and set out for the ruins.

AFTER GRANDDAD GOT whopped by that stroke and couldn't work anymore, Grandma thought she could revive his body and spirit with a testament to hard labor. During that summer of agony and woe, me, Grandma, and a sturdy team of men remolded the abnandoned lot behind the corner store into a lush garden.

It flourished for a while—it did—fat tomatoes and waxy bell peppers, all the flowers you could ever want. There were even designs on a peach tree, but we'd never see it. Try as we might, no miracles took root in that rocky soil. God's right hand closed over Granddad, crumpled him up like paper. Six months after he passed, God's left hand closed over Grandma, smothering the fire in her breast, reducing that lick of bright flame she called a tongue to a crackle inside my head.

Nobody knew what to do with the junk left behind, those barrel drum smokers, buckets of salt, and sacks of weevil-infested flour. Nobody knew the blood magic behind snoot sandwiches, or how to sew a life out of throwaway parts. So the corner store sat sagging and stagnant.

I had been avoiding that block where the corner store stood. I wouldn't even turn down that street. I couldn't. I don't know why. I don't know what I expected to see there, a crater, a black hole. I expected to find anything except for volunteers tending Grandma's garden.

A colorful sign that read BACON STREET COMMUNITY GARDEN had been erected in front of Grandma's rose arch. Grandma had wanted that rose arch to represent her children and grandchildren, each blossom a pulse. She would've gutted any fool staking claim to what she had built. Even though those volunteers willed spinach and hot peppers out of scarred earth, nurtured celosia into lashes of flame, I couldn't stop believing Grandma and Granddad's half-buried corpses fed that soil, phantasms sundered from flesh, thick roots gripping rib cages, pelvic bones. I couldn't stop seeing phlox surging out of their skulls, blooms studding eye sockets and gaps between coffee-stained teeth.

As I approached the garden, a white lady in a floppy wicker hat waved a trowel overhead and lectured a group of bored little kids. Little boys dueled with copper pipes or dozed, hugging shovels taller than them. Little girls compared and catalogued braid styles, whacked each other with slap bracelets, giggled madly. The lady croaked louder, thrusting her trowel, trying to intimidate and tame. Nobody listened.

I snuck to the back row of the garden where raised beds of collard greens grew. A rich vegetal musk rose as I snipped their stems and chlorophyll ran cool across my palms, highlighting life and love lines.

The lady approached and said, "Excuse me." She pulled that floppy hat tighter over her knobby head.

"Exactly what are you doing?"

The little kids *awwwwww'd* and whooped like sirens. At least they'd have entertainment.

I played it slick, kept gathering, and said, "Nothing at all. Just picking greens for dinner."

"I'm sorry, but you can't do that." She wrinkled her nose as if I stank—I probably did. That bone-deep summer heat and handling pounds of rank offal did me no favors. "This is a community garden. Anyone is more than welcome to the harvest if they put in their fair share, but I'm not sure I've ever seen you." She shook her head gently and tried to offer a pitying frown, but it crinkled into a tired scowl.

So I told her my name and where I lived and about Grandma and Granddad and a bunch of stuff about the corner store.

Her scowl flipped into the type of smile that cracks under pressure. "How nice!" She eased the Ziploc bag of greens out of my hands and sidled herself between me and the garden. "Let's make a deal: why don't you come back on Friday in clothes you don't mind getting a little dirty? We have plenty of alfalfa and cardoon to plant. It would be wonderful having a man who knows his way around this land."

I wanted to tell her the crop of greens I harvested were probably ones I had planted, grown wild and strong, and there was a red brick etched with my full name and birthdate somewhere near the alley, and I wanted to tell her about the fearsome growl of a chainsaw as it revved in my sweaty grip, the scream and whine of dead limbs, wood pulp in my eyes, and about how dull hatchets bust against tough tree stumps, and about the scars on my hands and knees, bleeding all over brambles.

I wanted to tell her about Grandma's hair, white and thin as milk-pod fluff, how she shriveled and sagged like rotten fruit, moaned and saw ghosts on her deathbed. I wanted to tell her I knew nothing about botany, but a drop of warm blood could feed spring blossoms through winters and winters and winters—goddamn—I wanted to tell her don't play with my intelligence. I wanted to tell her to get the fuck out my face. But I didn't know her like that. So I just shrugged.

The lady nodded approval. Those little kids sniggered, pointed at me. I loped away with my head hung low. I schemed. No barbwire fences protected the garden. No motes, no guard towers. I would come back at night, infiltrate Bacon Street Community Garden, take what was rightfully mine.

THE MOON HUNG overhead, slight and yellow. Heat lightning sizzled inside streetlights. Moths wobbled drunkenly through swampy air, collecting what nectar they could. Residual heat pumped off the concrete and steamed the soles of my ratty sneakers as I stalked inside the community garden, fearing a gruff voice would holler *FREEZE!* I'd spend the rest of that night in a cell with a deadly felon asking me *What you in for, lil' homie?* And I'd have to tell him *Rutabagas. I stole rutabagas and collard greens.* Dude would be like *Oh, for real? Nigga, you cold-blooded.*

I collected greens as dumb-ass rabbits darted underfoot, their furry rumps bounding across the garden. They romped with acrobatic grace then suddenly stopped and flattened out in the grass. The shadows loosed a stray dog, clawed feet beating, kicking up clods of dust. Those dumb rabbits juked and jived, scattered over a hill and vanished. That fool dog lunged after them, his long, red tongue flying like a war banner.

I yanked up a few beets, just to be ornery, and before leaving I searched for that brick with my name on it, wondering if it might contain a critical piece of my backbone. I picked through rubble and wiped away dust with my T-shirt, but found nothing. A high-pitched shriek sliced the viscous night. I caught a tang of iron on the stale, oily breeze. I scattered too, not wanting to be the next kill.

MY LUNAR CHARTS proved correct. Yell was back in her room when I returned home with a fistful of greens and soil. I could hear her spitting mean whispers into the cordless phone. I snuck across the floorboards, squatted in front of her door, and spied on her through the key hole. She ate those slimy flaps of turkey meat and chalky saltines. Between bites, she nodded her head and said *Right. If you ain't feeding me, fucking me, funding me, what good is you? Nah—I can't tell her that. I can't tell her nothing. Right.*

*

THE NEXT NIGHT I set out the good linen tablecloth. It rolled like a sea of cream in soft candlelight. Polished forks and plates and glasses floated atop lavish, milky waves. Daylight from the window drained and my shadow began to loom monstrous against the kitchen wall. I toiled over the stove, scanned Grandma's note cards for methods of damage control. I read Grandma's recipes thrice, followed them to the exact letter—I did, I swear I did— but the greens were brown, and the cornbread stony, and that tripe still looked hideous—like tripe—and the gizzards were hard as plum pits.

And then there were those chitlins.

Those awful, goddamned, evil-assed chitlins. I scrubbed and washed and rinsed, scrubbed and washed and rinsed, but once they started boiling, it stank like donkey-butt soup. So much worse than barnyard funk. Only an exorcism can rid a house of that stink.

I had confused desire with ability. Grandma's cooking was a dark and necessary form of alchemy. Her blood thickened the gravy. Her fat fried the fish. She ground her bones to flour, rolled biscuits with her marrow. Grandma's devotion was ascetic. How foolish could I be, trying to conjure her miracles in one manic night?

Frantic, I tried lifting the pot of chitlins off the burner with bare hands, blistered my palms, dropped it back in place. I was yowling when Mom tromped in with a rag over her nose. Yell followed a hot minute later. My failure had summoned them like a bell.

Mom and Yell were stunned by that foul odor. Once they made eye contact, their stances widened automatically. Nothing had been settled. Yell tied her hair into a tight ponytail, plucked out her earrings. Mom clenched her jaw, kicked off her flats. My body coiled, readied to spring between them. But that reek smothered all will to fight.

"Avery," Mom said, "what in the world is that stink?"

Yell grimaced and asked, "What died?"

I stammered the answer. "Chitlins."

Mom and Yell shook their heads, eyes dazzling with grim wonder. They lifted lids and adjusted burners, studying that food cautiously. Mom came to a hypothesis first, "Avery, please don't tell me you called yourself cooking dinner."

Yell smirked and said, "Oh my God. Boy, you could at least open a window." She rolled her eyes and relaxed. "That funk is making my hair frizz."

Mom broke a mean smile and said, "That stink is peeling my nail polish."

The oven timer beeped and Yell said, "Don't worry, y'all—I'll get this one." She couldn't hide her glee as she whipped on oven mitts and pulled out that pork tenderloin. It smoked and looked more like the mummified shank of a forgotten king than the Best of Anything.

Yell guffawed, and Mom said, "Oh Lord, please help us."

Mom and Yell chewed and spat out the greens, crushed cornbread in fists, told jokes: *Who taught him to cook, Wolfgang Yuck? Boy, you're bout the only one who'd get fired from a soup kitchen. Shoot, a bum couldn't eat this—that's cruel and unusual. Now, does this count as an act of terrorism? We don't need feds kicking down the door. Won't somebody please open a window? I am so serious—the damn drapes are burning.* Their contempt and mean jokes were good as cleavers against my throat. You can't make a meal or reconcile a feud without a little blood on the floor.

I snatched the oven mitts from Yell, hefted that pot of chitlins overhead, trudged out to the alley, and pitched them all over the cobblestones.

Pigeons fell out of the sky like rocks and cats slinked between chain-link fences. They fought over the best cuts, feasted on that mess. Looking over at the kitchen window, I could see Mom and Yell laughing their heads off, snapping tongs at each other, giddy as fifth-grade girls. I was mad enough to cry. But I knew they didn't enjoy this sisterhood often. Might as well let them have their fill.

SHINE

YELL BIT MOM on the shoulder, so Mom kicked her punk-ass out again. Then Mom made me put on rubber gloves and inspect the wound for signs of infection. I assessed the damage with a miniature flashlight and a magnifying glass. The wound was a perfect oval, as if Yell had attacked with a precision cutting instrument and not teeth. There was discoloration—red, green, and purple, like weather-beaten aluminum—but there was no pus, no gangrene. Funky tufts of fur didn't sprout from Mom's face, nor did she become a zombie.

One day later, Yell's stuff was jammed in garbage bags and boxes. Two days after that, Mom organized a yard sale. I lugged grimy folding tables out of the basement. Mom made placards, even busted out that fine and sophisticated calligraphy she learned at the Y.

She earned ten bucks off an old lady who haggled over Yell's antique hand mirror for a solid hour. Mom closed up shop when a crusty white dude with only 2.5 teeth in his head asked: *Got any gently used stockings? I'd take garters too.* Three days after that, Yell's stuff was back in her room, hair care products categorized by severity of kink, Freak 'Em dresses hung with respect. Two more days after that, Mom sighed and told me, "Avery, you need to go find your sister."

Why'd I have to go? I wasn't the one who put her ass out—and really—I was enjoying the peace. With Yell gone, I didn't have to referee fistfights or put up with her lousy boyfriends pissing on toilet seats, jerking off on the couch cushions, and calling me a scrub. Nor did I have to compile and catalogue the various death threats Yell attracted from ugly, bald-headed girls.

I wanted to spend my weekend playing video games, killing ogres and saving kingdoms. Not bumming through the streets looking for my dumb-ass sister.

Yell hated my guts anyway. She was forever trying to squash me under her thumb. When we were kids, she would punch me in the arm and, when I punched her back, she wailed like I had ripped her in half. Mom would braise my butt and make me stand on top of a milk crate one-legged, arms stretched out, heavy cans of soup in each fist. Yell mocked me in silence, her fake tears dried in salty streaks, a smirk that could cut diamonds beaming on her face.

I asked Mom once *What did I ever do to her?* Mom answered right away, like the question was an eventuality, same as sunrises, deaths. She told me *You were born, Avery. Stop breathing, and y'all might just get along.*

Mom's hyperbole was the grim truth. I could imagine the casket and my bloated corpse, cold and blue as a slab of beef from the freezer, my tie pointed and sharp as a blade. Yell and Mom would hold hands. Mom might whisper *I've never seen him so dignified . . . so handsome. Why couldn't he carry himself like this in life?* Then Yell would frown bitterly, throw chrysanthemum petals over me, sign the cross.

I figured looking for Yell was a waste of time, but I knew better than to tell Mom no. Her nerves were landmines. I had enough shrapnel in my chest. I sighed, added a slump to my shoulders, and said, "Will do."

She pulled an envelope out of her purse and said, "Be sure she gets this."

I stuffed the letter in my back pocket and prayed it was laced with anthrax, the dramatic end to an enduring mother-daughter feud.

Mom pouted a bit and said, "Thank you," which was unexpected and awesome, but then she rapped my chest and went back to commanding. "Now get, or you won't ever find her. That girl's slick and mean."

I WANTED TO believe Yell was slicing notched machetes through Amazonian flora as she tracked rare panthers, tarantulas scattering under her feet. I wanted to believe she was Kumite fighting in Thailand—a musty, concrete theatre bristling with blood-lusting spectators, adrenaline setting claws in her spine, she and the champ trading punches to the chest like masochists posing as sadists. I wanted to believe all that, but I knew she was most likely chopping it up with one of her dickhead ex-boyfriends, smoking dirt weed and guzzling cough syrup until the ghosts of dead prophets dropped from the ceiling and empty Pringles cans became megaphones heralding End Times.

She could've been with Big Boulder, a lunkhead who once held his breath for five minutes on a stupid dare and subsequently forgot everything he had learned in ninth grade—the imbecile believed babies are assembled inside a woman piece by piece through repeated copulation, and the union between numbers and letters is witchcraft. She could have been with Fly Ricky, a pretty dude known for having the silkiest hair and six baby mamas by the age of twenty. Or she could have been with Cal Rich, a roided-out, Adderall-pill-hustling party monster. Dude couldn't even grin without juicy veins breaking across his forehead. Neighborhood lore had it he drank so much protein powder whole biceps fell out the back of his ass when he sat on the toilet.

Last time Yell was out fucking with Cal Rich, he called me at two in the morning. The connection was fuzzy, overpowered by background noise, girls laughing like delicate, loopy birds, Pleistocene bass thundering, glass breaking beneath toxodon hooves. Liquor and hot musk steamed through the receiver. Cal grunted and told me *Come get your sister, homie. She wildin' harder den a mug.*

I found Yell on Cal's front porch, soupy vomit slicked down her chest, tank top and bra rumpled as if a blind man had dressed her in the dark. No shorts, no underwear, nothing covering her bruised thighs. Narcotic rage thumped in my head, made me woozy. I glared skyward, but the moon and stars offered no counsel.

I cracked the front door and glared inside. Cal and his boys raged, their party beach themed—white sand on hardwood floors, tatted up babes in neon bikinis, semi-automatic Super Soakers, fake palm trees rustling under box-fan breezes.

Cal's boys were all mini-Hulks, crossbred with bovines, unabashed gigantism in their blood. Any one of them could have devoured me in two chomps. And they were crazy as hell.

One dude did jump-squats with babes giggling on his back. He ripped into a smoked turkey leg between reps. Another was down on all fours, out-slobbering and out-barking a big-ass bulldog. They traded affectionate head-butts. For real.

Cal sipped something viscous and crimson from a golden goblet as he watched the festivities from his leather recliner. Carnal satisfaction softened his pulpy face. A brick smashed across his forehead would atomize into powder, wouldn't do him a lick of harm, and still I plotted an attack with kung-fu techniques, Swift Panther Claw, Thousand Lotus Palm Strike. Employing the proper use of ferocity, surprise, and a broken bottle, I could at least gut Cal before his boys stomped me into a subatomic particle. Bravado told me to *nut up*. Cowardice told me *she's not worth it*. Wisdom told me *the situation's not worth it*. Yell told me *ssshhhlllgrrrb*. I brushed a chunk of beef out of her hair. She said it again: *ssshhhhlllgrrrrb*.

I abandoned the offensive, took off my pants, and shimmied them over her hips. I hefted her on my back even though she reeked like a level-ten sewer slug. She drooled on my neck and asked *ssshhhhhlllgrrrrrbbb?* I snapped: *Fuck if I know. Don't ever do this dumb shit again. I will hunt you down and kill you myself. Swear I will.*

MOM'S LETTER SIZZLED against my butt cheek like a hot coal, but I didn't dare open it—what if it was sealed with a curse passed down by Egyptian queens? If I had transgressed boundaries, I thought I would be transformed into a toad—or worse yet—my balls would straight fall off, jiggle out my pants leg, get swallowed by a gutter—for real. It would happen to me.

An old man with rheumy eyes and one hand once told me *Ain't no sense meddling in the affairs of females. You won't fix nothing, and you might just get hurt.* He pointed his stump at me and said *How you think I lost my damn hand?*

Besides, I had to figure out which of Yell's busted-ass ex-boyfriends to challenge first. Fly Ricky could finesse me. Cal could hurl me over the horizon like a discus. But Big Boulder was easily confused by shiny metal and polysyllabic words, so I decided he could get it first. I loaded my backpack with essential questing items: cans of warm Vess, hard candy, two real ninja stars, and a wooden kama blade. I grabbed my bike and set out.

A lumbering Cadillac nearly clipped me as I glided past St. Louis Avenue, the driver's face dopey and apathetic with the latest kush. Miss Diamond was at her usual spot by GO! GO! Inn, raising the hem of a velvet dress, fabric curved like a bat's wing. I rode past dead zones, defunct storefronts, and buildings like sick men with twisted bones. Weeds tangled through my spokes. Honeysuckle exploded through chain-link fences. Wild chicory blazed ethereal blue. I turned onto Garrison and hit a filthy mess of kids playing freeze tag.

They romped, wheeled *YOU'RE IT* and *NUH-UNH* and swatted arms and legs as if a furious cloud of wasps had descended. Boys lunged, snatched bolos and berets. Girls broke into smooth, zebra-esque strides, hurdled over street cones and stone flowerbeds. My stomach was a cauldron, absolute jealousy and nostalgia mixing, sweet and poisonous. Me and Yell used to play. We swept ankles in hopscotch, aimed for faces in four square. I knew she'd rather maim me than lose a thumb war. Yet her voice always had some mysterious power over me, could cleave the dark and drag me back home.

As I rounded the corner and saw Yell sitting on Big Boulder's porch, chopping it up with two goons, I found my voice didn't have the same mysterious power over her. I glided to a stop and shouted her name, "Yell! Hey, Yell!" The goons gas-faced me. Yell crossed her arms. I shouted again, "Danielle!" But right then, she couldn't spare me the comfort of a familiar *fuck off* or *eat a sick dick and die*. She seared me with a look and stomped inside the house.

I stalked after her, past the snickering goons, ready to unleash my kama blade, sever necks and tendons, cut them down. The goons were silent and still, ugly as gargoyles. They spat no insults, raised no hands.

This just wasn't their fight.

YELL'S HAIR SPILLED over her face in copper spangles as she split open a strawberry cigarillo with a letter opener. She delicately broke up a nugget of weed, her fingernails sports-car red. She abruptly stopped processing the weed, cocked her head, and stared at me like I was an apparition in Big Boulder's trashy living room.

I cleared clothes, sporks, and dirty paper plates off the couch and plopped down across from her. "Where's your boyfriend?"

She shrugged and snorted. "Shit, I don't know. I ain't his keeper." She rolled and licked the blunt artfully. "He's probably out eating paint chips or beating his head against the wall—whatever it is mongoloids do."

She flashed a mean, toothy smile. I felt better, brave even. She sparked the blunt, took a sagacious rip, and spewed fluffy cumulous clouds of sticky smoke. She passed it to me. I ripped it and tried to hold a deep breath, but the smoke was coarse and harsh as wool, thrashing my throat and lungs. I sputtered thin vapors. Thick strands of slime oozed out of my mouth.

Yell retrieved a tall can of warm beer from underneath a couch cushion and cracked it open. "Damn, Avery—you weak as fuck. You got them baby lungs. Nobody respects a man with baby lungs, especially not a girl." She took a swig of beer and passed it to me.

I drank and ripped the blunt again. I fought the urge to gag, held in the smoke for a full three beats, and exhaled a respectable contrail. Tight cords in my shoulders and back slackened. That weed was no punk.

Yell grunted approval and snatched the beer back as a space-time tear opened in the living room. Me and Yell drifted through the cosmos, ashtrays over Andromeda, dirty sneakers and comets careening. Tall-can satellites.

"Hey!" Yell's voice boomed. "Hey, shit-for-brains!"

I banished the visions, sat up, and drawled, "What?"

"What do you mean, what? You the one up my ass. What do you want?"

My hands had become monstrously huge, the gnarly hands of a hobo-eating troll. I fumbled in my back pocket for Mom's letter and dropped it at Yell's feet. "Mom said you need to come back home."

Muscles in Yell's neck tightened. She'd shoot the messenger and jam his head on a pike, no problem. I thought about the dude with one hand and regretted taking this quest. I told her, "I guess you're supposed to read that letter."

Yell studied the letter like a lynx contemplating the best strategy for stealing meat from a snare. She started to stoop for it, then stopped and raised an eyebrow at me. She snapped, "What are you looking at?"

"Nothing."

"Stop looking at me then."

I obliged her, turned around, and listened as she slit the letter open. I craned my neck just a little and kept her in my peripherals. In her hands, I knew a dull letter opener would be enough to pop kidneys, carve vertebrae. I turned and saw she wasn't menacing, but reading thoughtfully, holding the letter open like a Dead Sea scroll, her lips moving.

Her expressions were rushed watercolor. Confusion bled into doubt; doubt bled into contempt; contempt bled into a cautious tenderness. Then she swallowed, huffed, and absently rubbed her belly. Thunderheads moved across her brow. She folded that letter over and over and bit her lip red. She tore the letter into pieces and threw it in my face. I expected this. No surprises there.

Since Yell broke the letter's seal herself I figured I was safe from testicle dismembering hexes. I kneeled on the floor, put the pieces together, read what I could.

Mainly there was Mom's lexicon of Eternal Judgment and Guilt:

Miss Danielle,
   This is for your eyes only. Go ahead & be trifling all you want to be – I can't stop you. You don't listen to a word I have to say. And all I'm saying is you need to do better. Is that so much to ask? Then you want to repay me with nastiness And th⟨...⟩'m not judg⟨...⟩say I'm not judging you.
I ⟨...⟩

Deadly blows to the head and heart. But mixed in with the lethal onslaught were slight words of encouragement:

And then there was that short list of random names:

Hot Damn!

RECKONING DISPELLED MY high. I saw clearly—I knew. I pointed at Yell and shouted, "Awwww, Danielle! You're—"

But she cut me off with a slice of her hand and said, "No."

I clenched fists and stammered. "What do you mean? You're—"

She sliced at me again and said, "No, Avery." Her lips were a flat, angry line, but her hands trembled—what could I say or do? If I tried hugging her, she'd power-bomb me through the coffee table. Beneath her meanness she was bony, lonesome, and weak. Everybody knew that much. She didn't need a soothing hand or kind words—she needed to feel strong. Strong enough for herself, strong enough for my nephew or niece.

A lunar belt of magazines and musty socks soared overhead as I ripped the blunt and schemed. Yell snapped her fingers in my face and hollered "Puff, puff, pass, shit-head." Then I got it.

I stubbed out the blunt and said, "I'll play you for it."

Yell crossed her arms and said, "What the fuck you mean you'll play me for it?"

I told her, "Like I just said. I'll play you for it." I opened my hands and beckoned. "C'mon, Hot Hands. You win, and you do whatever. I win, and I get to pick the name."

She tried to snarl, but her eyes were wet and unconvincing. "Boy, don't play—"

"No, c'mon. Rex, if it's a boy. Vanessa Laquisha Donetta Annette Delores Colt the Fourth if it's a girl."

"You're not funny."

"C'mon, play me." I snatched her hands. She didn't resist. "You know I'll whoop that ass."

She slid her hands under mine and said, "I go first." She flashed that sharp smile. "Oooo, boy, I will slap the stink off you."

We knew the rules. Best two out of three. Flinch three times and you lose. Winner mushes loser upside the head. Yell's offense was clever and brutal. She tickled the fat part of my palm and—*SMAK!* slapped my right. She jerked her shoulder and—*SMAK!* slapped my left. She hypnotized me with eyebrow dances—*SMAK! SMAK! SMAK!* She half-committed to an attack and made me flinch once.

I disengaged, shook the burn out my hand, reengaged, and—*SMAK*! She belched in my face—*SMAK*!

Either I had smoked too much or she had five hands. During a rapid fire assault, she faked me out two more times and won the game. She mushed me upside the head and hooted. My plan was sound in theory, but I had made one awful miscalculation: Yell always won Hot Hands when we were kids. By the time she was done, my hands looked like I had stuck my fist in a bowl full of fire ants. Welts bubbled on my flesh like air trapped in pizza dough. She'd laugh and call me a pussy, a loser, a punk-ass scrub, but I'd keep playing her and playing her until her hands looked just as bad as mine.

She won the next two games, easy. I would rather have been skinned with a dull straight razor than face her again, but I held my hands out and beckoned. I told her, "Best three out of five."

I would play the best twelve out of fifteen to give Vanessa Laquisha Donetta Annette Delores Colt the 4th a chance. Shared pain is a crux of love. Accepting scorn that cuts deep and nicks bone is the truest vow. Even though I'd never be the most faithful brother or uncle, I could do this one thing: offer my flesh and endure.

Yell rolled her eyes and popped her neck. She adjusted the chunky bracelets on her wrists, smirked, and took my hands in hers.

NOBODY PROMISED MILK AND HONEY

BEFORE THE CORNER store failed, Grandma used to sit out front and gut buckets of fresh catfish Granddad had caught that morning. Those catfish flopped over each other, fins slapping, mouths gasping, gills slicing open into long, red slits. She'd pull a paring knife from her apron, set down newspaper, and clean them right there on the curb. Sludge-dripping guts glowed in the sun, a clutch of bruised rubies. Once she had the fish frying inside, she'd stand in the doorway and hawk lunch specials. She'd be hollering *Come and get it! Come and get it! Fresh, big-lipped catfish straight out the muddy Mississippi! Hang a tooth on that cornmeal crust! Hot sauce and onions ain't never had a better friend! I said c'mon, y'all! Them pans is burning up! That grease is popping! Them catfish is jumping! Boy, is they jumping!*

TRUTH IS I wanted my first job to be at Grandma and Granddad's corner store, so I could rattle open those iron gates at dawn, fire up that oil-drum smoker, and squint as coals snapped a chorus. I wanted to shave cloudy chunks of ice for sno-cones, pickle hot peppers harvested from Grandma's garden, roast chicken bones and gizzards for that good gravy. I wanted to sneak rings from the toy machine to young kids and hope aluminum hearts might ward off misfortune. I wanted to ride my bike and deliver platters of snoots, neck bones, and ham hocks. I wanted to holler lunch specials at day laborers, bless lottery tickets, and haggle over dusty cans of sweet yams with mean, goat-bearded women who knew how to stretch a dollar further than Laffy Taffy. For real. I'd smooth wrinkles out of sweat-soaked dollars sourced from the heels of boots, the bottom of bras, ignore that damp funk, and praise working folks. At the end of each day, I'd douse the coals, rattle the iron gate closed, balance the books by dusk light. Grandma would peep over my shoulder while Granddad scraped burnt bone out of the smoker. She'd laugh bitterly, pop one of those pathetic bills, and tell me *Avery, boy, it's raggedy—but it's still money, ain't it?*

MISFORTUNE CRUSHED GRANDMA and Granddad before I had that chance to work with them. Without their sweat and blood, the corner store sat stagnant, fist-sized padlocks and burly chains locking the doors. The stress and financial burden from their passing kept me and my surviving family sick.

Mom couldn't work Dillard's cash registers since that thyroid condition walloped her. Migraines with nauseating halos overwhelmed her and caused what she called *The Second Coming of Motherfucking Jesus Christ Himself.* I tried to help out by washing dishes at King Candy, a diner that served chocolate malts and White Americana on the cheap. County folks braved trips to North St. Louis just to chomp patty melts and eye me with suspicion. Even though I worked like a dog, $6.50 an hour plus tips didn't help my situation. Danielle held down a good-paying job at a nursing home, but she struggled to fatten our family's coffers and also keep Jabari flush in formula, diapers, onesies.

At only three-months old, my nephew knew we were lacking. He judged the family's failures and puked oatmeal mush in disfavor. He puked when the lights flickered off, and I had to wipe his chapped, angry butt by candlelight. He puked when the refrigerator died, and I moved all of our cold cuts to a Styrofoam cooler. He puked when I tried to rig the water meter with a wrench, a pair of pliers, and a bag full of sand. Ain't nothing uglier than a baby who knows worry. Worse yet, I wondered if Grandma and Granddad were in their graves, pissed off and spitting at our mistakes. I wondered if Dad figured he was right to ditch losers like us.

I'm saying money had achieved real super hero status in my house. Andrew Jackson could swoop in with his paper cape whipping behind him, put pizza in shriveled stomachs, stock cabinets with soap and deodorant, resuscitate phone lines with his breath, put the spark back in power outlets, and beat back those muscular bills.

Those muscular bills flexed on us, talked shit better than professional wrestlers—ON THE 29TH I'M BREAKING YOUR CANDY-ASSES AND TAKING WHAT YOU OWE ME!!! Each bill hit us with a signature finishing move, The Car Insurance Crippler, The Natural Gas Suplex, but no slam could top the Funeral Expense Crucifix. Grandma and Granddad passed one right after the other, and the cost of services, caskets, and graves equated to thousands of dollars we plain didn't have.

They left behind no inheritance, no vault full of precious gems and gold that shone and vaporized gloom. But they did leave behind a mess of junk. Smokers, slicers, ranges, and other industrial kitchen equipment remained locked inside the corner store. Besides that, busted washing machines and piles of scrap from a doomed laundromat venture crowded our basement at home. After losing her job, Mom was finally desperate enough to try and sell all that rusty, dusty crap. She rubbed her temples and figured we might get lucky and find a big-ticket item, a generator, a jackhammer—something that would give us the sum of money and strength to power bomb those shameful funeral expenses through the floor.

ME, MOM, AND Danielle made our first descent into the basement as Jabari wailed himself to sleep. That place possessed every disquieting quality of a crypt. Dead men huffed cold breath on my neck. Wind muttered curses, conspiracies. Rats chewed mysterious chunks of gristle and observed me with contempt. I lugged beat-up washing machines from one spot to another, carefully avoiding holes in the wall, afraid a troglodyte might reach through and stroke my hair.

Even as high-watt bulbs softened the gloom, and organization provided simple comfort, I was unsettled by grim fantasies of what lay in the strata beneath the asphalt, beneath my feet, the crown and casket of a dead king, broken totems and war axes, jackal bones, canopic jars, a tribe of men crushed into blood-red diamonds. A corrosive strain of toxic grime colonized my fingernails. A dank sewer stink clung to my skin. One night after hours of mining the basement, I woke up coughing and expelled a whole, live moth. It levitated in the dark between my eyes, swooped, disappeared in a wisp of flame and smoke. For real. After weeks of superstition and toil, the basement remained elementally gross but was made neat enough, plunder displayed on long fold out tables.

We excavated all kinds of junk, rotary telephones, exercise bikes, power tools, musty clothes, dress shoes, pipes, door frames, costume jewelry, bullets, Granddad's World War II service revolver, Cabbage Patch Kids, traffic signs, and a mess of crooked keys. Not a pawnshop, not a fool would buy half that crap. But Mom had hope. Once our excursions were done, she raised a tarnished brass plate and grinned. She told me and Danielle, "Look, y'all. Bet I could hit this with vinegar and lemon juice, shine it up something fierce, flip it for 10.99."

While Mom and Danielle considered our spoils, I tucked Granddad's revolver in my waist band, swiped a fistful of grimy bullets.

PAWNSHOPS AND JUNKYARDS refused half of what Mom had to offer. Disappointment made her migraines meaner, nastier. She called me from a pay phone after hearing the one-hundredth HELL N'ALL and demanded that I sort out the corner store and catalogue whatever industrial junk might be valuable.

Mom told me, "I need you to get down to the store and do some cleaning. I can't be out here fussing like this. Organize too. Don't just make a bigger mess."

I held the phone in the crook of my neck and pulled Granddad's revolver from under my bed. Call me foolish, but I believed some small part of his soul suffused that chrome. I cocked the hammer, heard his knuckles crack. I squeezed the trigger, felt his muscles coil. I slapped and spun the cylinder. It clicked like a trading card between bicycle spokes—*TAT-TAT-TAT-TAT-TAT*.

"What's that noise?" Mom asked. "Avery, what is that noise?"

"Nothing." I spun the cylinder and slapped it closed. "I'm refurbishing a hand crank generator I found in the basement. For science class."

"Boy, don't get smart."

"I'm not. Dumb as ever."

"Whatever you say. Just get over to that store." She huffed into the receiver. Her breath burned my ear. "I'm not asking too much, am I?"

"No, ma'am."

"Put on gloves and a mask—new gloves and a new mask, not used ones—and please don't wear good clothes."

The line clicked dead.

LOSS FELT FRESH as I cleaned and organized the corner store after work each day. It took all my strength to pop that padlock, loosen those chains, slide back that iron gate, and step inside. The place languished in a shade of limbo. Walls had sponged up smells of cooking and meat and produce. That thick, stagnant air tasted like chicken stock and onion, grubby old potatoes. Sno-cone syrup bruised the tile and faux-marble counter tops. Brass buttons on the cash register sparkled sadly like commendation medals. Tables and chairs salvaged from the dumpster were littered with soiled napkins, cigarette ashes, and fish bones, the remains of phantom customers dining and dashing. Sun light blazed through filmy windows and banged off the stainless-steel slicer.

I appraised equipment and conjured visions of prosperity to ease the tightness in my chest. I saw Danielle taming a stove that hissed and grunted like a beast on squat hooves. I saw Mom managing the books, man-handling those burly, big-mouthed bills, knotting them up in figure-four locks, making those motherfuckers tap. I saw Jabari cooing in his bucket seat, charming customers out of coin for the tip jar. I saw myself slicing chunks of salami paper thin, taking out the trash.

My intrusions into the corner store disturbed spirits, broke protection spells. I worked each day in daze, dodging dull, restless phantoms, dueling guilt and shame. In difficult moments I spat prayers into the ether and offered my flesh to whatever would listen. I offered the fat off my back to fuel the fryer, the steel wool in my hair to scour pans, the blood in my veins to lubricate the slicer. But no angel accepted my gifts, descended through the ceiling, and kissed my forehead. No demon clawed out of the earth and offered me peace in exchange for that first taste of blood. So I prayed instead that my burdens would be incinerated into ash, that barbs would be plucked from my heart, that grief would lose its grip.

GRIEF ONLY THROTTLED harder when I biked over to the corner store and found folks in the middle of robbing the place for all that rusty, dusty junk. They even had the nerve to make a celebration out of it. Little boys and little girls wetted each other with Super Soakers, splashed water balloons. One girl wearing a frilly swimsuit whirled a hula-hoop around her plump belly, shook water out of her braids. Old men and old women congregated, held cold cans of beer to their foreheads, spoke on *what it is, what it ain't, what it never was,* and *what it always will be.* A painfully skinny man hunched over a tiny grill and flipped polish sausages, coals flaring and popping. A boom-box crooned sweet, classic R&B.

An old man shoved a hamburger in my hand and told me *Hey, now, grab you a bite!* Another old man said *Get you a beer!* But then an old woman said *N'all, he too young.* Then another old woman winked at me and said *He looks 'bout old enough to me. He fine too* and the first old woman said *Then give him a sip of yours, if you like.*

I ignored the offer and watched as a few sulky teenage dudes with ropes tied around their waists struggled to haul away Granddad's indoor smoker. Another pair strained to push Grandma's deep freezer through gravel and weeds. Three trucks idled in the alleyway, flatbeds loaded down with kitchen equipment from the corner store. A fast song rattled from the boom box. All the old folks and kids screamed, started jiving.

Now I've always been soft, the type of fool who will love those who wrong him, who will sing the songs of his transgressors, who will praise the wounded until flowers bloom from what's left of septum and soft palate, thick honeysuckle thrush. Those folks were just as worried, hurt, and desperate as me and mine. But I couldn't let them stunt and take what belonged to us.

I shouted—nobody listened. I shouted again—nobody listened. An old woman smiled, tried to take my hand. I pushed her away. She told me *I didn't want to dance with you no way, ugly.* I shouted a third time—nobody respected me. So I pulled out Granddad's revolver. An old man two-stepped in the dust. I cocked the revolver, aimed at the sky, squeezed the trigger. No report, just a *CLICK.* A kid busted a water balloon at my feet. I cocked the revolver, squeezed the trigger—*CLICK.* An old woman raised her hands and clapped. I cocked the revolver, squeezed the trigger—*CLICK.* Skinny asked *Now what in the world is all this?* I cocked the revolver, squeezed the trigger—*CLICK.* Vipers slithered through my brain. The world flashed ruby. I cocked the revolver, squeezed the trigger—*CLICK.* Fire crept up my spine. I cocked the revolver, squeezed the trigger—

A BIG FAT JUICY THANKS

Y'all—this acknowledgements section should be a thousand pages deep. I'll do my best in two pages. My deepest gratitude goes to the Saint Louis University English Department for offering patience and guidance during my undergraduate studies. Special shout outs to Vincent Casaregola, Victoria Casaregola, and Antony Hasler.

I don't know if I'll ever be able to fully express my appreciation for the faculty at the University of Missouri-St. Louis MFA program. John Dalton and Mary Troy, thank you for continued concern and advice. Shane Seely and Glenn Irwin, thank you for your insights. Howard Schwartz, thank you for asking me how much I would give to move forward. Steve Schreiner, thank you for saying what you do to these sentences isn't violence—it's love.

UMSL's MFA program has cultivated more than a few bright minds, and I'm grateful to Kenny Squires, Brigette Leschhorn, Angela Mitchell, Ryan Patrick Smith, Jason Vasser-Elong, Lauren Wiser, Marisol Ramirez, Jennifer Goldring, Gianna Jacobson, Jen Tappenden, and Emily Grise.

Big thanks to the editors at *Black Warrior Review*, *Draft Horse*, *Gulf Stream Literary Magazine*, *Natural Bridge*, *december*, *Midwestern Gothic*, *The Masters Review*, *SmokeLong Quarterly*, *Cog*, *Ninth Letter*, *Tahoma Literary Review*, *Black Warrior Review*, *Story Quarterly*, *Juked*, and *Pleiades* for maintaining publications that support fresh voices.

I find myself constantly amazed by the ferocity, talent, and generosity that exists in our writing community at large. Big thanks to Michael Czyzniejewski, Denton Loving, Michael Nye, Keith Lesmeister, Jodee Stanely, Ryan Ridge, Meagan Cass, Phong Ngyuen, Jessica Rogen, Shasta Grant, Gail Aronson, Reem Abu-Baker, Blake Kimzey, Donald Quist, Kim Winternheimer, Alison Syring-Bassford, Todd Summar, Noley Reid, James Tate Hill, Joe Ponepinto, and Keith Rosson.

With this book, I worked to enter vital conversations of identity, origin, and faith. Upon sending it out to initial readers, I was worried that I hadn't done enough, but the responses I received were

more than gracious—I feel as if I connected with kin. I only hope
to keep moving forward and make y'all proud. Big thanks to John
Keene, Danielle Evans, Rion Amilcar Scott, Steven Dunn, and Tom
Williams.

Much thanks to the editors and board members at *River Styx* for
putting up with my nonsense. Jason Lee Brown and Shanie Latham,
y'all the best.

Gaining support from the Regional Arts Commission to complete
this project was a huge honor. Thanks to Roseann Weiss, Saher Alam,
and Travis Mossotti for working hard to facilitate funding.

Extra special shout outs to Lindsay Daigle for being one of the
smartest poets I know and trusting me to speak at her wedding;
Soma Mei Sheng Fraizer for believing in me when I needed it most;
Ian O' Neil for being the best artist on planet Earth, and Joe Betz for
always chasing paper with me—IT'S LIT!

Of course this book wouldn't have been possible without James
Brubaker and the team at Southeastern Missouri Sate Press. I lucked
out in having the opportunity to work with James and benefit from
his talents and integrity.

Thanks to my family for teaching me how to get it.

Thanks to Jennifer Austin for her compassion and support.

Thanks to Elijah Austin for teaching me how to live.